I Told You So

I Told You So

By: Adrian Driscoll

Driscoll Entertainment

I Told You So LLC in association with Driscoll Entertainment
P.O. Box 57343
Los Angeles Ca, 90057

Co-Authored by Michael A. Williams
Cover Photography by Gene Avakyan
This book is a work of fiction. Names, characters, places and incidents are products of the author's imagination or are used fictitiously. Any resemblance to actual events or locales or persons, living or dead, is entirely coincidental.

1st "I Told You So" Paperback Edition October 2014

ISBN 978-0692313091

Acknowledgements

I truly wish I could name off everyone who had a part in making this project possible, but I'm afraid the list would be linger than the book. However, there are a few people that I have to thank. First off, **ALL GLORY TO GOD MY SAVIOR. WITHOUT HIM I AM NOTHING.**

To Mom – I grew up watching you struggle and strive to provide an amazing life for my sister and me. You are the strongest woman I have ever met, without your inspiration I wouldn't have come this far! You are an inspiration and I am genuinely honored to be your son.

To Sis - I have had the privilege of watching you grow up and helping raise you. And even after all of these years you still never cease to make me proud. You're an amazing young woman! Don't ever let anyone tell you differently. Don't ever stop your journey! Anything you want can be yours all you have to do is declare it.

To Mama D - I'm not allowed to call you Grandma because that's for old people. You have been the backbone of this family for all of my life. Without you I couldn't have become the man I am today. I am forever in your debt for that.

To Grandpa – I love you and I miss you. You taught me to be a man, to respect women and to love those around me.

Acknowledgments (Cont.)

To Peanut – They say behind every strong man is a strong woman. You are the fierce force that makes that saying true. I'm honored to be your man!

To My Team - Brian, Rahney, T-Bras, Davon, Brittain, Abby, Lee and a few others. I've known you basically all my life! Blood couldn't bring us closer. You have been loyal from day one even when I was at my lowest. You're the true definition of Friendship. DB4L

These Next few acknowledgements are special. Even though they don't know me...

To The Queen (Queen Latifah) - I first met you while I was audience on your show some time back. You've come so far and your positive energy is a HUGE inspiration to me. The love you spread is contagious. That's a rare and beautiful trait.

To Will Smith – Man I've never met you but I feel like I've known you all of my life. Your philosophies have been nothing less than inspiring. I've watched to your videos on YouTube a million times. You've constantly reminded me that ANYTHING is possible.

To Tyrese Gibson – Brotha, your book changed my life! I've gotta say you're the reason I gotten out of my own way and I am forever grateful for that. Keep inspiring people the way that you do. **God** has definitely given you a gift.

1

There's never a joy as special, innocent, and as free as watching two children running around playing. Best friends who have no cares, no worries, nothing stopping them from enjoying life in its fullness. The fact was, in that moment, the only thing of any significance to Michael was that he got to run away from Bridgette while she stretched out her arms, trying her best to catch and tag him.

"You're it!" Bridgette said, finally touching Michael's loose shirt.

They both stopped running for a few seconds and looked into the eyes of the other, smiling.

"No!" Michael cried, in disbelief, shaking his head arguing that he was now the chaser. "That doesn't count because you didn't touch me. You touched my shirt."

"You're just mad because you were caught by a girl." She teased.

He tried his best to look serious, but whenever he was with Bridgette a smile would almost automatically smear onto his face.

"You're still it until you tag me the right way." He declared.

"Really?" She questioned and then giggled as she quickly touched him on the skin of his arm and ran.

"Hey, come back here!"

The two of them ran aimlessly across the park grass until the sunset and the flicker of the streetlight indicated it was time for them to head home. Their interaction showed the brilliance of the friendship they would cherish for years seeming as though nothing would ever separate them.

"Race ya home," the competitive Bridgette exclaimed.

"Ok!" said Michael, "But this time I'm not gonna let you win."

"Yeah yeah yeah, just try to keep up." she teased.

2

One evening some years later, Bridgette was with Michael at his mom's house where the two of them had just eaten dinner to take a break from their unfinished homework. They sat next to each other on the large brown living room couch, working to complete an important assignment before they returned to school the next day.

"What did you get for number eight?" Bridgette asked.

"Um, forty seven and a half." Michael responded, his mind had been somewhere else the entire day.

"Okay," She nodded. "That's what I thought. I was just checking."

Bridgette looked back to the TV that had clearly been distracting them for the duration of the assignment, but Michael couldn't keep his eyes off of her.

Ten Years had passed since the two innocent children ran through the park chasing one another. Ten years for each of them to grow and develop their friendship and ten years for

Bridgette to change from Michael's competitive best friend to the love of his life.

Bridgette was a beautiful young woman. Her long brown hair flowed all the way down her back. Her skin was lightly tanned without blemish. Her brown almond shaped eyes were perfectly complemented by her long lashes. Her white and braces straightened teeth shone from beneath her protruding lips, surrounded by laugh lines, and two lengthy dimples on each of her cheeks.

As for Michael, he wasn't the type of guy that girls usually flock after. He kept his jet-black hair in a small messy afro. His beady black eyes were hidden behind a thick pair of tin framed glasses. Like most kids his age he fought with Acne and his white teeth rarely showed due to his sheepish smile.

"So are you sure?" Michael asked.

"Am I sure what?" Bridgette responded clearly confused.

"Are you sure you don't want to be my girlfriend?"

Bridgette giggled, believing it was a joke. She had already told him no numerous times before. "Stop playing around, Mike, if we don't finish this homework Ms. Vanderbilt is going to fail us."

"But I'm not playing, I'm very serious." A nervous smile attached to his lips. "Haven't you at least wondered—?"

"Stop!" she interrupted. "Please just stop, Michael."

"You really mean you haven't even considered us being together after all these years? You know how amazing it would be if we were a couple?"

"Mike, listen…" She paused because she knew what she was about to say would hurt him, but she also knew he needed to understand. "I love you, but only as my best friend. A relationship between us could ruin everything we have."

"I don't think it would." he argued.

"What if something went terribly wrong? It would be nearly impossible for our friendship to remain intact."

"That's a risk I'm willing to take."

"But I'm not." Bridgette said sternly.

An awkward silence hovered in the room. Bridgette couldn't believe Michael brought up the subject again when she's already told him how she felt so many times before. All she expected to do that evening was go to his house so the two of them could finish their math homework together, she didn't understand why they were having this conversation again. As for Michael, he didn't understand how she couldn't feel the same. Everything she said to him was valid, but his feelings for her were valid as well and he refused to believe they weren't going to be together.

"Bridgette—"

"Is that what you want Mike?" She immediately interrupted. "A thirteen year friendship poured down the drain?"

"People break up because they don't know each other well enough before starting a relationship. You said it yourself, thirteen years. How much better can two people know each other? I know everything about you, from what irritates you to knowing your favorite ice cream is Rocky Road. I also know it's nearly impossible for you to go two days without watching CSI and that you think animals are disgusting except for the little Teacup Yorkie things. And—"

"MIKE!" She screamed, clearly bothered by his continuous debate. "Please stop! I get it, you care about me. You know a lot about me and yeah, I guess it would be cool if you and I dated, but it's never going to happen. You have to quit asking me to be your girlfriend, because I'm never going to change my mind."

"You say never but just watch, you'll have my baby one day."

"What?! What did you just say?"

"You'll have my baby one day." Michael repeated hopefully.

"What the hell is your problem? I'm not having your baby, ever! And if that was your idea of a joke it was not funny. You need to understand that *US* is never going to happen. There will never be a moment where we look back and you say you were right and I was wrong, because it will not happen."

"But—" Michael attempted to interject once more, but was quickly cut off.

"Have you not been listening? There are no buts. I love you to death so I've dealt with this shit, but it's gotten old. Every week some new thought pops into your head about Bridgette and Mike! And now this? A kid? Are kidding me? That's not something to play with."

Michael sat there in silence. A mixture of thoughts both angry and sad ran through his mind. How could she not be in love with him? How could she not share the same affection that he has given her for the past 13 years? Who else in the world could care for her like he did?

Bridgette tried to go back to doing her homework, but she knew if she stayed in the room with him there would be an awkward silence that she couldn't bear to listen to.

"You know what? I should go."

Bridgette gathered her things and looked back at the teary eyed Michael. She hated to see him in pain, but their friendship meant more to her than he knew and deep down she was glad she got it off her chest.

"Look, I'm sorry" She began, but was soon interrupted by the defeated Michael. He felt horrible about what she said. But he couldn't show how bad he was hurting.

"It's cool, really. I'll see you tomorrow."

Bridgette grabbed her things and headed home.

That night, Michael lay awake in bed replaying the conversation in his head. He didn't understand what could've gone so wrong. "Why, Bridgette?" he whispered to himself. "Why can't you see that we are perfect for each other? Why do you always go for the guys that aim to hurt you? Why have I always been the one you come to after another guy breaks your heart?" He began to catalogue Bridgette's past relationships. "When Steve cheated on you, who was there? When Matt said it wasn't working out, whom did you come to?" Michael began to scream, punching his pillow violently. "What makes them better than me? Why don't you love me?"

"Michael?" His mother entered his room, her face riddled with concern. "What's wrong Son? You were screaming."

He took a moment to think up a lie. To his mother, him and Bridgette were already an item and he would never say or do anything to damage that perspective.

"Sorry Mom, I was um sleeping. I had a nightmare."

His mother looked at him with care in her eyes. "Are you ok?" she asked.

"Yeah Mom, I'm fine. Goodnight Mom."

"Goodnight Son." She cut off his light and shut the door. Michael pressed his cheek into his cool pillow and fell asleep.

3

The following day at school, Bridgette approached Michael as he stood at his locker talking to a friend. He almost looked as though last night had never occurred. He seemed happy, but Bridgette knew him better than that. He had always been able to hide his feelings from the rest of the world, but when it came to Bridgette, he might as well have been transparent.

"Mike," she called.

A smile sat on his face until he looked up and saw who called his name. It wasn't that he was sad about not hearing the answer he wanted to hear. He was upset because he realized that he might have gone too far. His over aggressiveness may have damaged her perspective of him.

"I'm sorry about last night. The way I reacted." She began. "I shouldn't have yelled."

"No, it… it's fine." Michael stuttered, pretending he wasn't bothered. "I wasn't in my right mind. You know how I can get when I'm tired." He forced a light chuckled.

17

"Yeah," She comforted with a smile. "I just didn't want to leave things the way they were, you know? It would have been weird."

"Yeah I know."

"And besides, you're my best friend." They both smiled. "So what are you doing tonight? She asked.

"No plans really. What about you?"

"The same. Not much going on."

"Well, you could come by if you'd like and we could Red Box it? He responded shyly. Even though she had said they were okay, the last thing he wanted to do was make her feel uncomfortable.

"Yeah, sure! We can do that." She replied cheerfully.

"What movie did—?"

"Hey Bridgette!" Dion, one of their schoolmates interrupted, as he leaned against the locker next to her.

Dion was one of the most popular kids at school. He was captain of the Basketball team. Tall, handsome and well built. His voice was smooth, deep, and convincing. His hair was always cut low and lined up perfectly. Dion was the type of guy that could get any woman he wanted and knew it.

"Hi Dion, how are you?" A smile arose on her face.

"I'm doing good, really good." He smiled, looking intently into her eyes. "You should come to my show tonight. It's going to be a lot of fun."

"Um," She hesitated, glancing at Michael. "I don't know."

"C'mon Bridgette, you don't have any bigger plans tonight, do you?"

Michael shrugged his shoulders, indicating that she should go. "I guess not—" Her voice trailed off.

"Okay, good. Here's the flyer, be there at nine. Bring your um, friends," He looked at Michael. "If you want."

Bridgette nodded and smiled.

"I'm looking forward to seeing you tonight." Dion said, lustfully smiling at the bashful Bridgette before continuing his walk to class.

Bridgette was still smiling when she turned back to Michael. "You don't mind do you?"

"Not at all," His voice lightened. "It will be fun."

"Yeah." She said happily. "Something different!"

The bell rang for class to start and Michael closed his locker as he took a step back. "I'll pick you up at 8:30?"

"Perfect!"

"Yeah, perfect." He forced another chuckle and headed to class.

4

Bridgette and Michael walked into the nightclub that Dion was performing at; they also brought Becca and Liz, two of Bridgette's friends from school. The venue was a small dusty bar that had been modified to have a dance floor. There was an area located in the back where the DJ fumbled with cords attempting to connect his equipment. There was also a small wooden stage with two microphones and an electric keyboard set up already. Six nights a week the club was for adults only, but on Fridays the owner opened it up for all ages and local bands were given a chance to show what they had. If of course, they had a following.

Bridgette scanned the room excitedly for Dion. Michael and her friends followed in her search. She finally spotted him talking to a small group of people who appeared to be other artists.

"Dion!" Bridgette called, waving her hand in the air. "Dion, over here!"

Dion heard her voice and walked towards her. "Hey B!" He said, "I'm glad you made It." he removed his shades slowly and dramatically as if to remind everyone of how smooth he was.

"I am too!" She threw him a smile and the two of them shared a long embrace. Michael cleared his throat to interrupt their moment. "Oh," Bridgette said bashfully, "These are two of my good friends, Liz and Becca. And of course you know Mike"

"Hello ladies," He smiled, intentionally ignoring Michael. The girls smiled back and Michael stared coldly at him.

"So Dion, are you ready for tonight?" Bridgette asked.

"Ready?" He replied as cocky as possible. "Girl stop playing. You know this is what I do. It's all I know. The real question is are you ready?"

The girls giggled as Bridgette responded. "Yes Dion, I'm super excited for you.

"Ok then, watch me work." Dion returned his sunglasses to his face and walked away.

The host chimed in to introduce the next act coming to the stage.

"Is everybody having a good time in the building tonight or what?" The small crowd of about 40 people clapped their hands and cheered in response to his voice. "Alright then! Well let's keep this show moving with the special young talent that's up next. I need everybody to get ready, get hype and get the fuck up for my man, D-MILLZ! Give it up y'all!"

Bridgette and her girlfriends moved eagerly towards the stage while Michael slowly followed behind them.

Bridgette grinned from ear to ear as Dion and two hype men walked onto the stage. Becca and Liz just gawked at Bridgette and her life filled smile, whereas Michael tried his best to contain his negative feelings toward Dion. It wasn't any personal quarrel that Dion and Michael had, but Michael knew what a womanizer Dion was. Plus, if any other man had interest in Bridgette it left a bad taste in Michael's mouth.

The three girls leaned in to have a conversation while keeping Michael out of an earshot.

"He likes you." Becca said.

"And he's cute!" Liz finished.

"I told you!" Bridgette agreed.

"And that smile—" Becca imitated Dion's smile bearing all of her teeth at once.

"It's gorgeous." Bridgette added. "He kinda looks like P. Diddy right?"

Liz shot Becca a look of disbelief. "Girl He ain't that cute." All three girls exploded into laughter.

"What's up everybody, what is up? How are y'all doing tonight?" The volume in the crowd arose as the energetic Dion spoke. "I go by the name D-Millz and I'm here for your listening pleasure."

The lights dimmed slightly and Dion proceeded to perform one of his songs. The crowd's energy erupted, everyone began to dance and sing along, everyone except for Michael. He listened to the lyrics, studying every word searching for a flaw. He also stared at Bridgette intently, hoping her reaction was negative. "How could she like such a scumbag?" He whispered under his breath.

Dion looked offstage towards Bridgette and her friends. He then grabbed Bridgette's hand and began reciting lyrics from his song to her. *"And when we see each other we hardly even*

speak, She say she a good girl, but she know that she a freak!"
Next he looked towards Michael in the background expecting
to see his face red with anger. But instead of the angry scowl
Michael had before, he was smiling.

He blew it! Michael thought to himself. *There's no way
Bridgette would ever fall for a guy who said those kinds of
things to her!* He looked at Bridgette victoriously. But to his
unpleasant surprise, she was enjoying every word of what
Dion was saying.

"And that's my time!" Dion addressed the crowd after
finishing his last song. The crowd screamed ferociously as the
host regained control of the microphone. "Whoa, whoa, whoa!
I know I wasn't the only one in the building that witnessed my
boy D-Millz killing the stage yet again. Wow, what an
extraordinary talent. He never ceases to amaze me!"

Dion walked off stage and straight to Bridgette with a
smile, but trying to look cool at the same time. "What did you
think?"

"It was amazing! Where did you learn to rap like that?"

"It's something I've been doing all my life? Never stop
never settle, right? I have to push myself to be the best."

"Well, it was great."

"What about you Mike?" Dion gloated, happy to rub the performance in his face. "What did you think?"

The last thing Michael wanted to do was respond. He absolutely hated the performance, especially the part where Dion rapped to the woman he loved. But he knew he could afford to lose his cool in front of Bridgette and her friends.

"It was good man, good shit."

"Okay, so what are y'all about to do now?" Dion asked. Everyone looked at one another confused. Dion laughed at their reaction. "Well, I know of this party spot we can all go to if you're down."

Bridgette and her friends exchanged glances.

"It's kind of—" Michael was going to say it was late, until Bridgette interrupted him.

"I'd love to go." She said eagerly.

"Can't make it, Mike?" Dion asked.

Michael didn't want to be anywhere Dion was. The simple sight of Dion made him cringe. But he knew better than to allow Dion any alone time with Bridgette.

"No, I can, I was just saying it's kind of..." He hesitated slightly to conjure up a lie. "...Kinda lame here now, its past time to leave."

"Okay then. Bridgette, you could ride with me if you'd like." Dion offered.

"Mike, you're going right?" Bridgette asked.

"Yeah." Michael said shyly.

"No, but thank you Dion, we'll just follow you there."

Dion chuckled "Most def, just try and keep up Mike."

The ladies laughed and headed to Michael's Car.

5

Dion pulled up to the brown two-story house and jumped out of his car. Michael and the girls followed. "Wow I'm surprised your car made it all the way over here." Dion yelled to Michael.

"We got here just fine" The insulted Michael responded. The group followed Dion towards the door. There was a faint thumping of music coming from inside, the crisp night air making Becca shiver. There were a few ladies hanging out on the porch with red cups in their hands smoking cigarettes.

The group made their way through the loud low-lit house. People were packed shoulder to shoulder, pressed up against the walls. One coupled sat on the stairs making out. Two guys chatted in the hallway about the Laker's game that just finished. The strong smell of Marijuana smoke filled the space along with a light grey haze. As they entered the overly crowded living room Dion was greeted by Miguel, a fellow Basketball teammate.

"Dion!" He screamed! "What's good man?"

"Oh, you know I'm just kickin' it. Dion replied, shaking hands with Miguel.

"How was the show?"

Dion laughed. "Is that a serious question?"

"Of course not." Miguel joked. "I know you rocked the stage as always."

"Bridgette," Dion called to get her attention. "Do you want something to drink?"

"I don't really drink." She shied away.

He smiled. "I was talking about soda, smart guy."

"Oh," She said, feeling embarrassed. "Okay then. Yes, I would like to get something to drink with you." They took a few steps toward the kitchen. "Mike, you don't mind keeping Becca and Liz company, do you?" She asked.

"Um, sure." Michael replied non-sincerely. "I will."

Michael and the girls attempted to have a conversation, but it was highly awkward. They had never really conversed before, because Becca and Liz were Bridgette's friends, not his. The only time they were in the same space was when Bridgette brought them around.

"Hey, don't we have Dr. Shaw's class together?" Liz asked Michael.

"Yeah, I mean I think so. You sit behind Ryan, right?"

"Yeah!" She smiled. "I actually like that class, but it's so hard to pay attention because of Ryan."

They shared a laugh.

"That's Ryan for you." Michael agreed. "He never quits talking! Always going on about either smoking weed or how high he is. I know in his mind, he's never in the same room that everyone else is." Michael and Liz chatted for about twenty minutes before he realized Bridgette had been missing for a while. He scanned the room for her but she was nowhere within eyes reach.

"Sorry," He politely said to leave the conversation. "I'll be right back. I have to go to the bathroom."

He made his way towards the bathroom hoping to run into Bridgette along the way. Finally he saw a familiar face. It was Sergio, one of his long-time friends from school. "Hey Mike! How you doin' man?"

"Sergio! Have you seen Bridgette?" The concerned Michael asked.

"Yeah man, her and Dion went upstairs a little while ago."

A horrifying image of a helpless Bridgette haunted Michael's mind.

"Dion, stop!"

"C'mon, just a kiss."

"I said no! Get off of me!"

"Quit fighting it." Dion yelled, pinning her shoulders against the mattress.

"Help!" Bridgette screamed. *"Somebody please help me!"*

"Nobody will hear you. The music is too loud...you're mine now!" Dion grabbed her hands and forced her to her back.

"You're hurting me!" Bridgette cried.

Michael rushed up the stairs and started opening bedroom doors. Behind the first door there was a couple making out. Panic struck his mind, as the image of the helpless Bridgette replayed in his head. Behind the next door he witnessed a couple having sex. "Get the hell out!" the girl cried, as the embarrassed Michael slammed the door shut. The words *"Dion Stop"* echoed throughout his brain. He opened another door and the room was empty. Finally, Michael heard

Bridgette's voice coming from the room at the end of the hall and he busted through the door screaming.

"Get the hell off of her!" He yelled, only to find Bridgette and Dion sitting on the bed listening to music playing from his phone.

"Mike, what are you doing?" Bridgette questioned.

"Um—" He was at a loss for words.

"Yeah, what the fuck?" Dion added.

"I just thought…" The confused Michael attempted to form a sentence. "You were gone a long time. I was just making sure—"

Bridgette interrupted his explanation. "Making sure what? That I'm not a slut and I'm not having sex with everyone?

"That's not what I said." He defended. "I was just saying that—"

"You need to leave." Bridgette interrupted yet again. Michael said nothing. He stood at the doorway paralyzed with sadness.

"Dion, could you take me and the girls home?"

"Yeah, I can do that. Just let me know when you wanna go."

"Could you take us now, I don't wanna be here anymore."

They walked passed Michael. Bridgette couldn't look at him in that moment, but Dion glanced and shook his head with pity. As she made her way down the hallway her heart grew heavy. She stopped and turned to Michael.

"Mike, you have to get over me."

"Can you listen, please?" Michael begged.

Bridgette shook her head, feeling as if she had just lost her best friend because of his own jealousy.

"Goodbye Mike." She whispered as she and Dion walked away.

Tears began to form in Michael's eyes. He stood in the doorway lost in thought. The words Bridgette had just said repeated over and over again in his mind.

"You have to get over me." Michael began to sob. "I've lost her!" He screamed, "I've lost the only one I ever wanted to keep!" Tears were now flowing down Michael's cheeks and face. His whole body flushed and he felt the urge to vomit. "How could she leave me?" Michael turned and ran down the stairs. He kept running until he was out of the house and in the middle of the street. He screamed at the top of his voice

"BRIDGETTE!" But Bridgette was gone, Dion was gone there was nobody to hear Michael's cry. And with nothing else to do the broken Michael drove home.

6

The following Monday Michael hoped that things would be back to normal between him and Bridgette. He would apologize and she would forgive him. He would explain how he knew to control his jealousy now and she would be his best friend again. Sadly that wasn't the case.

Michael spotted Bridgette and Becca standing next to a set of lockers talking. "Hey Bridgette!" He said excitedly as he walked up to her. Bridgette didn't respond. She just continued talking as if Michael had never approached. "Hey Bridgette!" Michael repeated attempting to get her attention. She turned around and stared at him with a cold gaze. Her eyes were filled with disappointment.

"I'll see you in class Becca." She said, as she grabbed her bag and left. The defeated Michael looked to Becca for some sort of explanation.

"You embarrassed her Mike." Becca started, "And in front of Dion of all people. The best thing for you to give her at this point is some time to think. You gotta get over her Mike.

Sorry." She put a comforting hand on Michael's shoulder as she walked away.

Michael didn't want to believe it was possible that Bridgette needed time away from him. But he took Becca's advice and removed himself from Bridgette's life.

7

Much time had passed since Michael and Bridgette's last exchange of words. He had made many attempts to contact her after that night, most of which were subdued by her mother answering her phone and saying she wasn't available. After a while Michael quit trying all together. The hardest part for both of them was they would hear about everything the other was doing in life. There would constantly be a mutual friend that assumed the two were still inseparable who gushed about what Bridgette did or what they heard about Michael.

Bridgette missed her best friend but she would never look to engage contact with him. As for Michael, she was all he ever thought about. He had never stopped loving her over the years, but he'd been able to subside the thought of being with her. He had his own life now. He was in a relationship with a beautiful woman named Courtney, he had a decent job and he had earned his bachelor's degree. Bridgette was doing fine as well. She was working at a coffee shop as a barista. She was now dating Dion and she had never been happier.

On this day, Michael was anxious as he nervously held the phone after dialing Bridgette's last known number. He wished for some insight, but there was no telling how she'd react after these three years that passed.

"Hello?" Bridgette answered.

"Wow!" Michael smiled. "It's so good to hear your voice!"

"Who is this?" She asked.

"Don't tell me you don't recognize my voice."

"Mike?" She asked dumbfounded.

"Yes," He chuckled. "It's me."

"Mike! It's been so long! I've missed you!"

A huge smile painted Michael's face. *She missed me too! He thought to himself. "I knew she would! Okay Mike, play it cool.*

"Hello, Mike. Are you there?" She questioned. He cleared his throat.

"Yeah, it's been three years…and I've missed you too!"

"Has it been that long already? How are your Mom and Courtney?"

"Everyone's good, real good."

"Hold on Dion, I'll be right there." She called out. "Hey Mike, I gotta go but—"

"Bridgette wait!" He interrupted. Nervousness ran through his entire body, He swallowed hard and finally forced out his question, "I... I was wondering if we could get dinner soon, you know, catch up?"

"Yes, of course." She said happily, "That would be amazing! When?"

"Um, for me any day. When would be good for you?"

"Tuesday would work." She said.

"Then Tuesday it is. We can meet at Luigi's on 4th. 8pm sound good to you?"

"Sounds awesome. You don't know how excited I am."

"Same here. Just make sure you bring your appetite."

"You know I will." She laughed.

"Ok, see you then."

Michael hung up the phone and he had only one thing in mind. Even though he was with Courtney now, he had never stopped loving Bridgette. If she saw him now, if she saw how

much he had changed and how successful he had become she
would have no choice but to love him.

8

Michael arrived at Luigi's 30 minutes early. It had been Bridgette's favorite restaurant since they were young and his one goal for the night was to impress her. He knew this could very well be his last chance to make Bridgette love him again. He nervously went over the scenario in his head. Bridgette would walk in and say, "Oh my God Mike! You look amazing!" They would share a long embrace and both sit down. He would tell her stories of his college successes and *wow* her with how he rose through the ranks at his job. She would sadly confess how miserable she was with Dion and how she realized what a piece of shit he really was. They would have wine and reminisce over how much fun they used to have in school. They would get lost in the hours as they shared a delicious meal and they stared deep into each other's eyes. And finally Bridgette would admit that she should have picked him over Dion. How she would do anything to have another chance to make Michael and Bridgette work. Finally being the compassionate man that he was, Michael would forgive Bridgette and they would share a long passionate kiss and leave the restaurant together.

He sat at the booth nervously waiting for Bridgette to arrive. He glanced down at his phone to check the time when he heard a female's voice. "Good evening," a wave of nervousness flushed through Michael's face as he looked up. "Would you like to order something to drink?" The smiling female server stood in front of his table with her notepad open.

"No um, just water please." The disappointed Michael responded. He looked back down at his phone; it was 8:30 now and still no Bridgette. He took a sip of his water and thought to himself, "Did she really stand me up? Wow it really must be over."

"Mike?" Bridgette called as she walked up behind him.

"Oh my God. Bridgette!" He smiled. "You look great!" he said as they embraced.

"You look good too." She said holding him tight.

"Please sit." He insisted. "It's been forever, how are you?" Michael moved over in the booth, making room for Bridgette to sit next to him, but she took a seat across from him instead.

"I've been good and you?"

"Me too." He couldn't stop smiling.

"So what's new?" she asked.

"Not much really." He paused. "I'm still working at the base.

"Really, that's awesome! How's Courtney?"

"Oh, um…She's doing well. How is…what was his name again?"

"Who Dion?" She offered. "He's amazing, hardworking like always. Sometimes he'll be out working for three days in a row."

"I don't know if I would call being away for 3 days amazing." He said half-heartedly and they shared an awkward laugh.

"So, what are you craving? I'm starved."

"I already ate," Bridgette replied, "but maybe dessert?"

"Alright, well you know this place has the best selections."

"I know." She laughed. "You didn't have to remind me of that. You of all people know I love this place."

"Yea…" He smiled and handed her the menu.

In another part of the restaurant, on the outside patio Brad, a drug dealer that worked for Dion, was attempting to make small talk on his failing date with a beautiful young lady named Margaret.

"Your steak sir." The waitress placed Brad's food on the table before him.

"Thank you." He said in his heavy Armenian accent. A creepy smile crossed his face as he checked out the pretty young server as she walked away. He lit his large cigar and took a huge puff. Margaret waved her hand in front of her face attempting to make the smoke dissipate. "So Margie, are you into sports?" He said returning his attention to her.

"No, not really." She answered.

"No? You should be. You don't know how good a cigar taste until after a good jog. Ya' know, I went to a Lakers game once, and I sat so close that the goofy dumb ass what's his name? Um. Mbenga. He almost fell right into my fucking lap. Can you even imagine the price of those tickets?"

"I bet they were pricey."

"Pricey! Try $1500! Each!"

"So, do you go to a lot of these games?"

"No, I just took this broad with me on a date. She wasn't feeling it though I mean the better I was treating her the more she was trying to act weird—" His words trailed off. Another girl had caught his attention, but this time it wasn't for him. He saw Bridgette on a date with another man.

"Brad?" Margaret called but he wasn't paying attention to her anymore.

"Um, excuse me for a second. I'm going to the jon."

Brad snuck around to see whom Bridgette was with, stopping near the bathroom to call Dion.

"Hello?" Dion answered.

"Hey, it's Brad."

"Man, I know who it is. What do you want?"

Brad stuttered. "N-now you know I don't talk bad about bitches, but this girl is with another guy."

"Why the fuck are you bothering me for?" Dion responded annoyed. "I'm kinda busy at the moment." He turned to the woman he was with and said "Just one second baby."

"I'm not fucking bothering you, I'm not talking about any bitch, it's your bitch." Brad responded defensively.

"What? What are you talking about?"

"Your girl, Bridgette."

"Okay, what about her?"

"I'm at a restaurant and I see Bridgette on a date with some dude."

"What!" Dion screamed. "Who is he?"

"I don't know some light skinned dude. They're laughing and having drinks."

"And you're sure it's her?"

"Yea man, I know what she looks like. Do you think I'm dumb or something?"

"Where are you?"

"It's that place Luigi's, on 4th street."

"Stay there."

"Ok!"

They hung up as Brad snuck up behind the booth, out of sight but close enough to eavesdrop on Michael and the cheating Bridgette.

They had been engaging in a great conversation for over an hour now, reminiscing on old times and playing catch up with each other's lives.

"…And then Mr. Williams' hair piece landed on your desk and you screamed because you thought it was a rat!" Michael said laughing.

Their connection was as if they had never lost touch, but they had their own lives they needed to follow. Maybe the two of them falling apart would give them an even stronger relationship, Michael hoped.

"You know, I was actually worried about how this was going to be, us seeing each other again." Michael confessed.

"How come?"

"Sometimes when people don't see each other for a while, things can get... awkward."

"You're silly. It could never be awkward between us."

"Yeah—" Michael's voice trailed off as he thought of the last time they had spoken.

"I forgot how much fun we used to have. We would talk about just about anything for hours on end." She admitted.

"Yeah I know. We were practically, inseparable." Michael added.

An awkward silence hovered in the air. The two friends hated what had happened between them, but this was a second chance for both of them.

"I guess that's part of growing up huh?" Bridgette asked.

"Yeah, I guess so…" Michael paused and gathered his courage. This was the chance he'd been waiting for. "Well, we could be close again? It's not like we have anything to lose. We could hang out, you know just chill. You know, I'm not as much of a nerd as I used to be."

"You will always be that nerd!" She teased and they laughed together.

Brad raced to the door to meet Dion as he entered the restaurant.

"Excuse me sir, do you have a—" The receptionist began but Dion ignored her completely.

"Follow me, they're over here." Brad said as they marched in the direction of Bridgette's table. Dion stared in disbelief as he walked up and saw his woman with another man. Rage built in his heart as he looked at the two having dinner.

"Baby!" Bridgette said smiling, genuinely happy to see the fuming Dion. She stood to give him a kiss and hugged him tight.

"What's going on?" Dion said, taken back by her reaction.

"You remember Michael from school, right?"

He took a second to think and then a smiled molded onto his face. He suddenly realized that Bridgette wasn't on a date; she was simply having dinner with an old friend who posed no threat to stealing his woman away.

"Yeah, glasses, I remember him. How's it going kid?"

"Hi." Michael responded shyly.

"So what brings you here baby?" Bridgette asked.

Dion shoots a glance at Brad then quickly thinks up a lie.

"I, um, came to grab a bite to eat, but when I saw your pretty little head I had to come say hi."

"You're too sweet."

Dion and Bridgette kissed once again. Michael covered his face with his hand. He couldn't bear to watch the exchange. He was once again heartbroken and Dion noticed.

"So, Dion," Michael said half-heartedly, "How are things?"

"Things? Things are great! Making so much money I don't know what to do with it half the time. What about you, Mike? How are things with you? Still work at the base? You're a janitor or something, right?"

Michael shook his head. "No, actually I'm not a janitor, I..."

"Oh my bad." Dion interrupted condescendingly, he turned his attention back to Bridgette. "B, I gotta be honest with you. I didn't just come here to get food."

"Then why baby?"

"I came just to tell you that I love you."

"You're too sweet. I love you too baby."

As they embrace again Dion's eyes were locked on Michael.

Michael sat embarrassed, angry, upset, and sad. He caught eyes with Dion who was enjoying every moment of his pain. Michael wanted to wipe the smirk off of Dion's face but he knew that he couldn't do anything to embarrass himself in front of Bridgette again. In addition, Brad hovered over him watching his every move, waiting for him to do something out of line.

The restaurant stood quiet, as the exchange had caught everyone's attention. People watched eagerly to see the next event unfold. Suddenly, Dion got an idea that would destroy Michael for good.

"Bridgette," Dion smiled, removed the ring from his pinky finger, and dropped to one knee. "I want you to be my wife."

Tears of joy built in her eyes and eventually started to fall. A proposal was the one thing Dion had left to offer her and it finally happened. She felt her life was finally complete.

"Dion! Wow, oh my..." She was so happy that she almost forgot to accept. "Yes! Yes! Yes! I will marry you."

She embraced Dion passionately, her hands holding the back of his head as they kissed. Everyone in the restaurant clapped for the new engagement, everyone except for Michael. His heart sank into his chest and his eyes began to water. He tried to speak but no words would form. Michael couldn't believe Bridgette couldn't see through Dion's facade. This was all a ruse, an act, and it would be a huge disappointment to Bridgette if she went through with it, but she couldn't see it. She never had.

"Let's get out of here." Dion said to his new fiancée. The two clasped hands and walked out the front door, neither of them even stopping to look back at the broken Michael.

"Your check sir." Michael looked up and found the waitress holding their check in the leather bill wallet. He handed her his debit card and left.

9

Later that night Michael pulled up to the local bar. It was a hot spot on weekends and he figured some kind of human interaction would be good for him. Normally there would be a roar of music and conversations. But on a Tuesday night there were only a few people sprinkled throughout the venue. Two men stood at the pool table arguing over whose round it was. An older couple sat in the corner having wine. Another man sat at the bar watching the Miami Heat play vs. the San Antonio Spurs on TV. A tall skinny man stood behind the counter shining glasses. Michael sat down at the bar and put his head on the counter.

"Long night at work?" The bartender asked Michael, observing that he was nothing less than torn apart.

"Something like that." He responded.

"So what'll it be?"

"Tequila man…Leave the bottle."

The bartender laughed. "I can't do that, but it doesn't look like you'll have competition filling your glass again."

"There's always competition for me, it's always a contest!" Michael mumbled, thinking about Dion. "He doesn't even do it to win, he just does it so I lose! He doesn't care about her, he doesn't love her…All he cares about are his drugs!"

"Look man, I was only kidding."

"So was he." The tone in his voice lowered. "He doesn't want to marry her and I know she doesn't want to marry him. This isn't even about love anymore."

Michael's thoughts continued to be spoken aloud and the bartender wasn't sure what to say. "I—"

"I appreciate it, but don't even bother man." Michael drank a shot of tequila. "Just don't let the glass get dry."

"You got it chief." The bartender said, he refilled Michael's glass and walked away.

Michael took another shot. The few people in the building stared at him as he vented, telling the most recent story of his life to an audience that never requested to hear it. The bartender spoke to him every now and again, but it was mostly because of his concern of safety for the few bodies in the building. Michael took shot after shot until the bartender finally interrupted him.

"Hey man, you want me to call you a cab?" The bartender asked. "It's last call."

"No, I'm okay. How much do I owe you?" Michael asked, his words slurred in drunkenness. The bartender handed him his tab to close out. As he examined his bill, it reminded him of Dion. Matter of fact, everything seemed to remind him of Dion. "$140 bucks? I bet it's nothing to Dion, so it's nothing to me either? That piece of shit!" Michael opened his wallet to retrieve his debit card and it wasn't there. He searched every slot in his wallet but it was nowhere to be found. Next he searched his front pockets and then the two back before checking his wallet one last time. Still nothing.

"I just had it." He said to the bartender confused,

"You're fucking kidding me right?"

"I'm telling you I just had it two seconds ago."

"Sure you did," The bartender said as he motioned to his security guards to throw him out. One of the guards grabbed Michael by the left arm and exchanged a glance with the bartender. The guards brought him to the alley out back and one proceeded to punch him while the other watched. They beat him up until he was bloody and had no fight left in him.

He laid there on the cold pavement, seemingly lifeless, face first in the disgusting dirt filled puddle that was left from the rain the night before. At this moment, Michael believed his life couldn't get any worse.

10

Eventually Michael made his way home. It was about 4 am when he finally reached his front door, fumbling his keys trying his hardest to figure out the right one to turn the lock. He finally stumbled through the entryway drunk as drops of blood scaled down his face onto the carpet beneath his feet. He collapsed at the doorway.

"Oh my God, Mike!" Courtney frantically reached out to comfort him. "What happened?"

"Don't touch me!" He snapped.

"Mike, what's wrong?"

His eyes began to water from the sheer thought. "What's wrong? Everything is wrong. She's going to marry that piece of shit!"

"Who are you talking about and please tell me what happened to you?

Michael's emotions flailed inside his heart and through his body until they couldn't be contained.

"Bridgette—" He started, but was overwhelmed by his tears.

"Mike please talk to me!" Courtney begged.

"Okay." Michael finally responded and he told her the story of his night. Courtney listened silently, holding back her emotions of anger and sadness as the love of her life sobbed over another woman.

11

Later that morning Michael apologized to Courtney for his behavior. He swore to her that he was over Bridgette and his emotions the night before were simply fueled by alcohol. He readied himself for work, self-assured that he would be able to get through the day and not worry about Bridgette. Deep down he knew this was impossible but he would do his best to try. He ate his breakfast, said goodbye to Courtney and left the house.

While driving to work a flurry of thoughts ran through Michael's head. He could still see them as the two kids running through the park trying to tag each other. He still remembered his mother calling Bridgette his "Little girlfriend." He reminisced on them growing up together and watching movies. In fact it seemed as if every memory that they have ever had together was still crystal clear. But none of them as clear as the vivid memory that haunted him. The fact that just a few hours ago the girl he loved was stolen from him.

Michael drove faster. He knew if he got to work he could force himself to be distracted, even if only temporarily. But something caught his eye. To the right of him was an old building with its door open. The sign above it read *"Lucky's Pub, Open Early."* He pulled into the parking lot and turned off his car.

When he got to the door of Lucky's he took a moment to check his pockets to make sure he had grabbed the cash from his dresser drawer. The last thing he needed was something else to remind him of the night he just had. He pulled out the crumbled up wad of bills and went inside.

For the next few days Michael was in a routine. He would awake from his sleep, brush his teeth, and get ready for work. But after he left the house he would head straight for the bar. Work reminded him of Bridgette. Just about everything reminded him of Bridgette, but this bar just reminded him of the last time he got drunk.

After a week, Michael's routine changed all together. Instead of getting up, and preparing himself for the day, he would wake up grab a beer and sit on the couch. He wouldn't talk to Courtney; He wouldn't answer the phone, he would just sit on the couch watching whatever came on the television.

"Mike, please talk to me!" Courtney was saddened seeing him like this. "I'm worried about you."

Michael didn't respond, he just sat in the living room wearing his dark blue robe, socks, and boxer shorts. He didn't comb his hair or brush his teeth, he just sat there.

The house phone continued to ring and there were multiple messages on the voicemail. Finally, Courtney hit the play button, hoping that hearing messages from people that loved him could help.

He tried to ignore the sounds of the concerned callers. The first message was from his boss: *"Mike, we haven't heard from you in three days. Let me know if everything is alright."* The next was from his friend Sergio: *"Dude, hit me back man and let me know what's good"*

"I'm getting tired of this…" Courtney began, talking as Michael listened to the never-ending messages. "You need to get help because I'm not sure how much longer I can take it."

Then there was another message from his boss, *"Mike man, I'm really sticking my neck out for you here. I don't know what you're going through, but you need to get over it."*

"We need to talk—" Courtney tried again but Michael just ignored her.

The last message he heard wasn't from the one person he wished it were. It was his boss for the last time sounding disappointed: *"Mike, I tried to prolong this as much as possible, I really did. You were a good hard worker so this is hard for me to say, but your habitual truancy leaves me no choice. I have to let you go. Your last check will be in the mail on Friday."*

Before nightfall Courtney made a sound decision about her future with Michael. She loved him and she hoped one day they would be together until death do they part, but the feelings he had for Bridgette convinced her that Michael didn't have much more love to offer.

"I can't do this anymore." She said, her eyes full of tears. Michael looked at her, nodded and returned his attention to the television set. Tears flowed down Courtney's face. "Just so you know I'm leaving tonight. I'll be back for the rest of my things soon." Michael sat there non-responsive.

Courtney packed a few things and went to her mother's house, leaving Michael on the couch, the one place he seemed to find comfort. The phone continuously rang until he couldn't take it anymore and he screamed.

"I'm done!"

He ran upstairs and put on a pair of jeans. Then hurried to the pantry and took out a half empty bottle of whisky. Finally, he stopped by the closet, grabbed his jacket and left the house.

12

Fuck all of this! Michael screamed as he walked along the side of the narrow road. "Bridgette doesn't want me! My job doesn't want me and now Courtney doesn't even want me. Well fuck it! I don't want me either!" He took a drink from the glass whiskey bottle. "Why would they want a guy like me? A guy that opens doors, and pulls out chairs? A guy that remembers birthdays and never cheats! Why want *that* guy when you can have a guy like Dion. A piece of shit that makes you do what the fuck he says and has side girls and puts you in danger? A guy who only sees Bridgette as a fucking trophy! Well guess what Dion? You win!"

Michael continued walking until he reached a narrow bridge lit by a few yellow streetlights. He took another drink from his bottle and proceeded to walk. "This is where you go when nobody wants you right?" He said to himself, stumbling as he made his way to the railing. He peered over the edge and saw the dark river beneath him. The water stood still as pieces of paper and debris floated across. "Trash." he yelled, "This is where the trash ends up. You threw me away Bridgette!" He took the last drink from the bottle and smashed it into the ground. Michael had finally reached his breaking point.

As he readied himself to jump, Michael took out his cell phone to call Bridgette. She needed to know why he wasn't going to be around anymore. She needed to understand where she should've been all along. He dialed her number and put the phone to his ear. One ring. Two. Three, and finally her voicemail. *"Hey it's Bridgette, leave me a message."* He hung up in a rage. "Great, now she won't even answer my call." He put his phone back in his pocket and climbed onto the cold metal railing. "Say Goodbye to good ol' Mike." He said, as he peered into the jet-black of the water beneath him. "I won't be missed."

Just before he jumped, his phone rang. A familiar ringtone that had been only designated for one person. "Bridgette!" Michael screamed as he reached for his phone. Tears flowed from his eyes as he answered.

"Hello?"

"Hey Mike! I have so much I need to tell you!"

"Yeah Bridgette, I need to tell you some things too. Listen…"

"No no, me first! I have so many things to do for the wedding. I need to get my dress still and of course there is the color scheme I need to figure out and don't even get me started on the guest list…" Michael listened as Bridgette gushed on about the wedding. He listened to every detail as she went on about what she needed and how it had to be perfect. She was happy and her happiness was truly all he ever wanted.

"Well Mike?" Bridgette questioned,

"Huh?" Michael answered. He had gotten lost in his own thoughts and stopped paying attention to the conversation.

"I asked if you would be my maid of honor. I know it's unconventional but it's supposed to be your best friend and nobody knows me better than you do."

"Wow, Bridgette. I would be honored. Hey can you hold on a sec?" he asked, as he carefully climbed down from the railing of the bridge. Michael knew that if anything could destroy Bridgette's happiness it would be losing her best friend. *So what if we can't be together?* He thought to himself, *she's happy and that's what I care about.*

Michael walked home talking to the ecstatic Bridgette the whole way. Even though he realized they would never be an item, he had gotten his best friend back.

13

The light of the sun peeked into Michael's bedroom window. He struggled to open his eyes. His head throbbed from the night before. "Courtney?" he called, but there was no answer. He sat up in his bed and searched the room for her. But she was nowhere to be found. The only evidence that she had ever been there was a small pile of her laundry in the corner and the picture of the two of them that sat on his dresser.

"Wow, she's really gone." The defeated Michael sighed. So much happened in the last week and it was all a blur to him. He fumbled around the top drawer of his nightstand for the bottle of aspirin, took two and walked to the living room.

He plopped down on the couch, thinking how just the day before that very couch was a place of misery and discontent, but now it was a place for rebuilding. *Well, first I gotta get my job back.* Michael thought with confidence. *It shouldn't be too hard; Mr. Jenkins has always liked me.* He picked up his phone and called his work.

"Hi Janelle, can I speak to Mr. Jenkins please? Yeah I'll hold" he waited eagerly for his boss to answer.

"Mr. Jenkins! Just the man I needed to talk to."

"Hello Michael," Mr. Jenkins answered. "Look if this is about your job, sorry but I can't help you."

"But you know how hard I've worked for this company. One mishap shouldn't be enough for you to abandon me."

"Michael you disappeared for a week. You couldn't pick up a phone? Or send a message, an email, anything! Do you know how bad that makes you look? Or even worst, how bad that makes me look. And I still took a risk and tried waiting for you. What you did was very irresponsible and unforgivable in this company."

"I was going through a hard time in life, but I have gotten my life together. Please, Mr. Jenkins, Please—"

"You're a good kid, Mike, so stop begging…the truth of the matter is your old position has already been filled, so I couldn't do anything even if I wanted to. You already knew there was a line out the door of people waiting to take that spot."

His words left Michael lost. It couldn't really be over after one mistake, could it?

"There's really nothing you can do?" Michael pleaded.

"No, there's not. I can't just create a position for you."

"But, I'm willing to take any position offered."

"Mike, I've already told you I'm sorry, I really am. There's just nothing more I can do for you at this moment." The conversation grew uncomfortable. "Look, I have a lot of work to do. Take care Mike." He hung up the phone.

"Yeah, take care." The disgruntled Michael mumbled to himself as he hung up his phone. *Okay Mike stay calm.* He thought to himself, *I just need to find another job, but first I need to find something to eat.*

He figured he could borrow a little bit of money for food from his friend Sergio.

"Hello?" Sergio answered.

"Hey man."

"How's it going bro?"

"Times are tough man...Courtney left me and I lost my job. You think I could borrow 20 bucks?"

"Shoot man I'm broke, you know I would if I had it."

"Well, do you know a quick way I could get some money?"

"Yeah, I know a way, but it might be a little morally challenging."

"At this point, I don't care. Just don't get me thrown in jail."

"Nothing like that man." Sergio laughed. "You want me to come get you?"

"Yeah, if you could."

"Ok, be there in twenty."

"Thanks, see you then."

Michael wondered what Sergio had in mind. He was known for doing off the wall things to get money. But Michael also knew how important it was to get enough money to hold him over until his last check came in the mail. The last thing he had to fix was his relationship with Courtney.

She's gonna hate me! He thought. *She's probably not even going to answer, or if she does answer she's just going to tell me what a piece of shit I am for not trying harder to keep her. Or worse what if she already has another boyfriend?* Insecurities buzzed around his head as he forced himself to pick up the phone and call her.

"Hey Courtney." Michael said as she answered. "Can we talk—?"

14

The day finally arrived where Bridgette was to marry Dion. It was a happy day for Bridgette as she was on the verge of doing what she had dreamed of since she was a little girl. The purple and white ribbons streamed throughout the church. A buzz of conversation rose from the crowd filled with family and friends. The organ player played waiting music as the ceremony began.

Bridgette eagerly waited for her cue to come out. Her bridesmaids, Liz and Becca, assisted her with her dress assuring everything would be perfect.

"I can't believe you're getting married in less than twenty minutes." Liz offered with a smile. "And to Dion of all men."

"Yes, we're so happy for you!" Becca added. "It took you long enough. I thought you two would have had grandkids by now." She said jokingly.

Bridgette shot Becca a look and smiled. "I'm just happy it's here. I wasn't sure if it was going to happen after a while, but when Dion showed up at that restaurant and proposed I was completely caught off guard."

The wedding planner entered the room, "It's time Bridgette, are you ready?" "I think so." She answered nervously.

The organ player began to play the wedding march. Becca and Liz took their places behind Michael at the altar. "How does she look?" He asked with a half-grin. "She looks great!" Becca replied. The moment was bittersweet for Michael. He knew the importance of this day for Bridgette. He knew that if he did anything to ruin it in any way she would never forgive him. He also knew that the woman he loved was about to be completely unattainable. But more than anything else, he loved how happy she was.

Her snow-white dress hung to the floor, dragging through rose petals. Her face veiled in white chiffon. The wedding march played as she stepped through the smiling crowd that stood to her sides. The flower girl walked before her dropping white and lavender flower petals at her feet. Her father stood at her right side in his all black tux, a small lavender boutonniere on his left lapel.

Dion wasn't as focused on the moment as Bridgette was. As he watched her walk up the aisle his thoughts were on the woman he had sex with the night before at his bachelor party. *Damn she was fine!* He thought to himself, a huge smile of satisfaction painted across his face. *She was a freak too!* He glanced at his groomsmen and nodded, assured that they were thinking about the night before as well.

Finally, Bridgette arrived at the altar and her father awarded her hand to Dion. Dion unveiled her face and took a look at his blushing bride-to-be. He smiled and asked, "You ready B?"

Bridgette replied, "Yes Dion! I couldn't be more ready."

Michael gazed at Bridgette. She was beautiful, he had dreamed of the day he would be by her side at her wedding but he thought the circumstances would be quite different. *I'm supposed to be in Dion's place.* He thought to himself. That had been his thought process for the entire ceremony, but when Bridgette looked at him for approval he smiled at her reassuring her that she looked amazing.

"We are gathered here today..." The minister started, commencing the wedding. Michael stood at the altar uneasy.

His palms felt as though they got sweatier after every syllable the minister uttered. Bridgette delivered her vows. Michael refused to listen; he couldn't bear to hear her speak that way about another man. Dion delivered his vows. Michael kept his head down, only glancing every so often until Dion's vows were coming to a close.

"I love you Bridgette and I won't let nothing or *no one…*" Dion emphasized shooting a glance at Michael, "Come between us all the days of my life, because only I deserve you." Michael clenched his fist as the minister proceeded. Finally, the minister gave Michael his chance to intervene. "If anyone can show just cause to why these two cannot be lawfully joined in Holy Matrimony, let them speak now or forever hold their peace."

Michael felt everyone look at him expecting him to make a fool of his self again. It was as if they all knew he was going to kill himself, like they all knew he loved Bridgette, like they all knew he was waiting for the opportunity to stop the wedding because he didn't think it was right with the world. Finally Bridgette whispered. "Mike!"

Michael couldn't believe his ears. *She really does want me to stop the wedding.* He thought to himself, *she needs me to save her from Dion!* He smiled at Bridgette and right before he was about to speak she whispered,

"The ring, I need the ring."

Bridgette hadn't been calling to Michael for help. There was no distress besides the fact that he had forgotten to hand her the ring right after her vows. He reached in his jacket pocket and pulled out the gold wedding band.

"With this ring I be wed" Bridgette said putting the ring on Dion's finger.

"With this ring I be wed" Dion mirrored Bridgette's actions.

The minister smiled and delivered his closing words.

"By the power vested in me by God I now pronounce you husband and wife. You may kiss the bride."

■■■■■■■■■■■■■■■■■■■■■■■■■■■■■■■■■■■■■■

Two Years Later

■■■■■■■■■■■■■■■■■■■■■■■■■■■■■■■■■■■■■■

15

Dion and Bridgette walked through an indoor mall holding hands. They had fought the night before and typically whenever they would get into an argument it was followed by a trip to the mall. This was Dion's way of apologizing without admitting any fault. This was also his way of showing off his trophy wife. He loved the amount of envy that generated when he walked around hand in hand with Bridgette. Men would stare at her from a distance and gawk at the woman they could never be with.

Bridgette knew she turned heads but she only had eyes for Dion. She dressed very conservatively. She didn't show her cleavage and every skirt she wore was below her knee. Yet whenever men saw her they were instantly attracted to her. It may have been her energy that they found magnetic. Bridgette was truly happy. The honeymoon phase was over and her and Dion fought all of the time, but in her eyes she had her perfect life with whom she saw as the perfect husband.

"What you think of this watch?" Dion asked Bridgette as they walked by a jewelry store window. He pointed to a gold Rolex with diamonds on the dial. "Don't you have that one babe?" She asked.

"But this one has a blue face, it's a little different." He said in defense. "You know what? Never mind? You're right. My jewelry game is already on point."

Bridgette smiled and continued browsing for a store worth visiting. A tall stocky man headed in the other direction walked by her and checked her out. He smiled as he went about his way.

"Hey man," Dion screamed. "What the hell is your problem?"

"What?" The guy responded, a startled smirk on his face.

"You heard me...I said what the hell is your problem?"

"Uh—" He started, at a loss for words.

"You see me holding her fucking hand don't you?"

"Yea dude, I was just—"

"You were just being fucking disrespectful." Dion interrupted.

Dion's rules for looking at Bridgette were clear. If he didn't see that you were jealous, he figured that you must have an agenda to try to get her. And the last thing he was going to do was give up whom he considered to be his prize possession.

"Dude, chill." The guy pleaded.

"Aye man, don't tell me to chill." Dion was furious. "How about I break your fucking jaw?"

"Baby, just let it go!" Bridgette begged.

"What you mean let it go? You're sticking up for this dude? You know him? You wanna be with him?"

"No Dion! I'm just saying it's not worth it."

"No, it's not worth it for you to say another word Bridgette. How about you just shut the hell up?" Dion said, before directing his attention back to the guy.

"Now get the fuck outta here!" He screamed.

The guy said nothing, just stood scared and silent, before walking away with caution.

"Look, I didn't mean to talk to you like that." Dion apologized to Bridgette. "But you know better than to stick up for someone I got a problem with...I'm supposed to be your man. Now say sorry."

Bridgette's eyes watered, she hated to anger Dion and she knew how he was.

"I'm sorry, Dion."

"Good, I'm glad you understand."

He took a brief second to gather his thoughts. *Nobody's gonna try to take my lady from me!* He thought, looking at Bridgette. *She's mine and mine only.*

Dion spoke again, "And as I am your man, what is a man's number one purpose in life?"

"To make money, Dion." She had heard him say it many times in the past. Nothing was more important that making money.

"Nope, to make babies." He said with a smirk on his face. "I think it's time for you to have my seed."

Bridgette's face lit up with elation as she replied, "You're ready to start our family?"

"That's right." He nodded.

"Dion, I would love to have your baby."

"Well then let's go get to work." He said grabbing her hand and leading her to the car.

<u>16</u>

Dion sat on the living room couch waiting for Bridgette. About 3 Months had passed since they had decided to have to have a baby and they still hadn't conceived. Dion wanted a child but not as bad as Bridgette did. This was something that had been at the top of her list of wants since she was a little girl. She walked out of the bathroom with the pregnancy test in her hand, a look of despair on her face.

"Still nothing?" Dion asked after seeing her clearly saddened expression.

"Nope." She confessed.

She plopped on the couch next to Dion and leaned her head on his shoulder for comfort. Reality was trying its best to bring her down. Thoughts swarmed her mind that she would never be able to conceive a child.

"Dr. Daniels said he would call me back later today to let me know of some ways to become more fertile."

"Alright, well let me know what he says." Dion rose from the couch. "Imma take a nap," he said leaving the room in frustration.

A not so patient Bridgette waited for the doctor to call. Every minute in waiting felt more like an hour. A few hours later she received the call.

"Hi Dr. Daniels." She said excitedly.

"Hello Bridgette, how is everything?" The doctor responded.

"I'm doing my best to remain optimistic, but it hasn't worked as great as I'd previously hoped. I still can't conceive and I've done everything you've told me, but still nothing."

"Well there are a few more ways to help you conceive."

"Anything! Just tell me what I need to do."

Dr. Daniels cleared his throat. "Well it starts with your husband. If I recall correctly, you did say he smokes. Is this true?"

"Yes, he does."

"Could you let me know what exactly he smokes?"

"Um—" Bridgette was hesitant to answer as her voice trailed off.

"Bridgette, you have no need to worry. Doctor and patient confidentiality, remember? Everything either of us says will never leave my lips, Okay?"

"Thank you." She still felt a little reluctant to say anything, but deep down she knew she could trust him. "He smokes weed." She confessed. "But it's only because he's always stressed."

"Well," You could still hear his pleasant smile through his voice. "That could be the solution right there! Studies have shown that smoking marijuana can lower the amount of sperm a male can produce. The best solution would be to talk to your husband and ask him to quit smoking, then perhaps the two of you would be able to conceive."

"Really!?" Bridgette was very pleased to hear such an easy solution to their problem. "Thank you so much Dr. Daniels! I'm going to go tell Dion right now."

"OK, goodbye now."

They hung up and immediately after, the excited Bridgette ran into the room to tell Dion what she had just been informed.

"Baby! Baby! The doctor just gave us great news!"

"What is it?" He asked still half asleep.

"He told me it's a possibility I haven't gotten pregnant yet because weed lowers a male's sperm count. I was thinking maybe if you stop smoking, at least until I get pregnant then we might be able to..."

"Excuse me," Dion interrupted, an angry expression across his face. "What the fuck did you say to me?"

"I was just saying—"

"Oh, I know what you were saying. You're saying this is my fault?"

"No, baby, it's nobody's fault. I—"

"Are you stupid?" Dion leaped out of the bed now face to face with Bridgette.

"I didn't mean it like—"

Bridgette knew at that point there wasn't anything she could say to keep him from being offended. Each word she said only seemed to add more gasoline to the fire within him. Dion grabbed her by the sides of her shoulders and forced her back against the wall.

"Don't you ever talk to me that way!" He yelled.

This was the most afraid Bridgette had ever been of Dion. He had gotten angry many times before but usually over something smaller. Usually she was able to calm his anger with an apology and a few kind words but this time there was something different in his eyes. Dion was hurt. His hands went from her shoulders to her throat as he choked her.

"Dion, stop!" Bridgette begged but it did no good.

"You always make me hurt you." Dion said as he threw her on the bed and mounted himself atop her. Again, he wrapped his huge, strong hands tightly around her neck, choking her.

"Don't you ever again say this is because of me, you got it?" She attempted to force out a word but the most she could do was nod her head. He slowly released his hands from her neck and she gasped for air. It had only been about 2 minutes since she had walked into the room with what she thought was amazing news; and now Bridgette was trapped in a room with a raging psychopath.

"Do you see what you made me do to you?" He screamed, his breath reeking of alcohol. She nodded. "Don't make me do this ever again. I don't like doing this to you."

"I'm sorry." Bridgette whispered still barely able to speak as she still fought for air.

"You should know when I do something like this to you, it hurts me more than it hurts you."

She nodded. "I shouldn't have said that Dion. I don't know what is wrong with me."

"As long as you understand. You're sure you understand?" Dion inquired studying Bridgette's horrified face.

"Yes Dion, I get it."

"Good, now take off your clothes."

The startled Bridgette looked blankly at Dion's face. His eyes glazed with a combination of drunkenness and anger.

She slowly unbuttoned her shirt, then her pants, followed by the last few pieces of clothing she wore. He watched victoriously as she undressed. His pride wanted her to see that it wasn't his fault. In his mind, he couldn't have been the reason she wasn't getting pregnant. He removed his pants, inserted himself and violently began to thrust.

Bridgette covered her mouth with one hand. Mascara stained tears flowed down the side of her face and onto the pillow. A combination of fear, pain and worthlessness overcame her entire being. She lay there as Dion selfishly pleasured himself with her body and she did not move for fear of making him angry again. *This can't be love.* She thought to herself. *You don't do this to someone you love.* Dion suddenly stopped, looked Bridgette in the eyes and said, "That's how you make a baby." He pulled up his pants and left the room, a reassured smile on his face.

As Bridgette lay on the bed sobbing and motionless, her thoughts of the happy family that she wanted ran through her head. Her heart loved Dion while her mind hated him as of that day. The last thing she ever wanted was to be was one of those women who stayed in an abusive relationship. And although she knew she was wrong for following her heart, Bridgette had always been a firm believer that the heart was always right.

17

Michael struck a match and lit a white candle. This was the 100th white candle he had lit tonight. The aroma of freshly cut red roses filled the air. Soft jazz music scored the entire evening. He had sprinkled rose petals over the floor of the living room and bedroom. A bottle of fancy champagne sat on ice on the kitchen table. He took pride in the amount of work he did to make nights like this special for Courtney.

She opened the door and called out to him. "Mike! Honey?"

"Hey, my love." He answered.

"What is all of this?" She asked. She was used to Michael being romantic. He would leave random flowers and other signs of his affection all the time. He would still open doors and pull out chairs for her, but this time was more than he had ever done before.

"I have big news!" he said, a huge smile painted across his face. "I got a promotion! You are now looking at the new office Manager. It's more money and of course a bunch of other opportunities."

Courtney screamed with excitement. "Oh my God Mike! That's awesome! I'm so excited for you! I knew you would get it."

"Thank you baby" he responded shyly. "Now you know, there is a position that needs to be filled. And it's available immediately."

Courtney's smile quickly turned into a frown. She was insulted at his audacity. "Um Mike, I don't want your old job."

He smiled nervously. "No, not that one, it's the wife position. You interested?" He put his shaky hand into his right pocket and pulled out a small black felt covered ring box. He opened it and bent down onto his left knee. Courtney's face flushed and tears flowed down her cheeks.

"Will you marry me Courtney?" Michael asked.

"Yes!" She choked out. "Yes Michael. I will marry you!"

The two embraced and kissed passionately.

Michael ran to the kitchen and grabbed the champagne to celebrate. "A toast," he said as he popped the cork. He poured the gold champagne into the glass flute and handed it to her. He then poured himself a glass and raised it in the air. "To the woman that made me better than I ever dreamed I could be. I am honored to be able to call you my wife-to-be. May we grow old together. I love you Courtney!" With watery eyes they both clinked their glasses.

18

"Bridgette!" Michael screamed into the phone. "She said yes!" His excitement overflowed to tell the news to his best friend.

"What?! You're going to get married? That's insane Mike!" Bridgette said, happy for him. "How did it happen?" She asked only halfway paying attention. As Michael went over the details of his engagement, Bridgette's thoughts were on her inability to conceive.

"And of course I want you to be my best man Bridgette." Michael said finishing his thought.

Bridgette focused again, "Wow Mike, I really wish I could but I don't have the time. We're having some serious issues over here."

"Issues?" He asked.

Bridgette went on to tell the issues her and Dion were having getting pregnant. She explained how the whole process was really hurting their relationship. She told him everything that had happened with the exception of Dion choking her.

"And that's why I really don't have time to do all of the planning that is required of a Best man. I hope you understand, Mike."

"Yeah, of course," Michael said sadly, one of the most important things in the world to him would be for Bridgette to be in his wedding.

"But you will still be there right? You'll definitely come?"

"Of course I'm gonna be there! You have my word Mike."

"Ok good!" He sighed with relief.

19

Failure continued to plague Dion and Bridgette. They had attempted to conceive for almost six months now. Dion grew more and more on edge. He wanted a child, not tomorrow, not in a month or a year, but right now. His built up frustration showed most when he was drunk and he seemed to be drinking even more frequently than before. He wouldn't hit Bridgette but every episode made her believe that he eventually would.

The phone rang and Dion answered. It was Brad, calling to see if they had been able to get pregnant.

"Nah, my dude…Still nothing." Dion said, frustrated.

Bridgette heard his tone, walked near the doorway and eavesdropped on his side of the conversation.

"Well, she says that she's been trying, but I know that bitch is lying."

She listened silently to every word Dion said.

"That's exactly what I said... She's probably taking birth control or something...I know one thing though, if she's not pregnant soon I promise Imma kill her—"

That was all Bridgette needed to hear before she stopped listening and snuck away from the conversation to make an urgent phone call.

The phone continued to ring until Dr. Daniels answered.

"Hello?"

"Dr. Daniels, thank God I reached you. It's Bridgette Ross, I really need your help."

"Sure Bridgette, is everything OK?"

"I really need to get pregnant."

"You *need* to get pregnant?" the doctor asked, confused.

"No," She chuckled nervously. "I meant want to...please tell me if there's *anything* else I can do?"

"Well, Bridgette, there is this process that some couples do when having fertility issues. It's a lot more common than you might think, but I'm not sure it's what you're looking for."

"Could I come hear about it?"

"Yes, of course. Just come down to my office and I'll explain it to you."

"Thank you so much Doctor. I'll be there right away."
Dr. Daniels sighed. "Ok, I'll see you soon."

20

Michael looked in the mirror and straightened his tie. He pulled out his cell phone to check the time. It was 11:45am 15 minutes until he was going to marry the love of his life. He thought back how he had wasted so many tears and time chasing after Bridgette, praying, hoping and believing she would one day realize he was the right one for her. The way he went about everything was what shocked him most. There were so many regrets of things he said and did over the years in wake of his expectation, that even he would have considered himself pathetic.

None of it mattered anymore though. This was a new day, he had a new attitude, the sky was clear again and his heart no longer wandered about on its own without consulting him anymore. His thoughts now belonged to another, Courtney, who would soon take his last name.

The wedding was starting and while Michael was no longer obsessed over Bridgette, he still worried about her, especially on his wedding day. She wasn't anywhere to be seen. She had promised she would be there and she had never broken a promise to him. *She's probably stuck in traffic or something.* He said to himself, pulling out his phone. *I'll call and see where she is.*

"Hey Mike, what's going on?" The half-asleep Bridgette answered in a raspy voice.

"You forgot!" He said, disappointment projecting through his voice.

"About—?"

"Bridgette, my wedding is going to start very soon and I don't know if I'll be able to hold it any longer."

"Oh my God, Mike! I'm so, so sorry."

"Where are you?"

"I'm at home—"

"You aren't even dressed, are you?"

"No, I'm sorry. I totally forgot it was today."

"That's okay, I know it's not a priority of yours."

"Mike, don't be like that."

"Like what?" He said angrily. "Are you gonna make it or not?"

"You're going to hate me." She hesitated.

"No, it's fine really." There was no way to mask his disappointment.

"I'm just going through so much right now."

"Well then come get your mind of it. You and I both know I need you here."

"No, I can't. I'll just bring down your happy day… But call me tomorrow, okay? I have big news I want to tell you."

"Yea, okay."

Michael sat on the phone in disbelief. Never in his wildest dreams would he imagine that on his wedding day, one of the most important people in his life wouldn't be there. He was sure she would come to his wedding after he had sat and watched her marry a man that wasn't him. And nothing would have stopped him from being there even with all of the problems he was facing.

"Promise me you'll call me?" She pleaded.

"I will."

"Michael, promise me…I need you."

"I promise."

Sadness was in her voice as she prepared to say goodbye. The guilt of what she had done to Michael weighed on her. With tears in her eyes she continued.

"Go! Go enjoy your day…don't worry about me, alright?"

"Bridgette, I—"

"Don't…just go, and say hello to Courtney for me."

"Yea…"

Michael was at a loss for words as he hung up the phone. He had no way of figuring it out, but his gut told him something was wrong. He thought about it while walking to tell the reverend and the wedding planner it could start. He wanted to talk to Bridgette, but nothing was as important as watching Courtney walk the aisle to him in her beautiful white dress.

Once Courtney reached the altar, she knew what was bothering him.

"She's not coming is she?" She whispered while the reverend spoke to the crowd.

"It isn't important." He lied to her, not wanting to stray his thoughts away from the two of them. "It's just me and you right now. That's all that matters." He grabbed her hand and they both shared a smile.

The wedding commenced.

21

The sound of the commentator's voice echoed throughout the house. "Kobe Bryant with the basketball, he shoots, HE SCORES!"

"That's my dude Kobe, best player in the game," Dion said, as he sat on the couch, his eyes glued to the television. He reached for his beer on the coffee table. This was a typical scenario for Dion lately. He would be unattached from the world for hours at a time, until he found it was time to consummate with Bridgette. The thought of a baby seemed to be all that was on his mind.

Basketball, aside from drinking was Dion's getaway. It was all he'd ever watch on television because mostly everything else was irrelevant to him. He watched every game the Lakers played. This was his time to himself and Bridgette knew not to interrupt him unless she wanted to hear his mouth. Halfway through the second quarter, an overwhelmingly happy Bridgette arrived home and entered the living room where Dion sat.

"Baby," She began. "I have great news!"

"In a minute…I'm sure you can see the game is on!"

"But Dion, it's important."

"It can wait until halftime." He demanded.

"It won't take long."

He shot Bridgette a cold look, irritated by her persistence.

"Please!" She begged, offering her smile as a bribe. "I promise it won't be time wasted."

He turned off the television.

"Okay Bridgette, what was so important that it couldn't wait until halftime?"

She ignored the annoyance behind his voice. "I'm Pregnant!"

"What?" Dion said in amazement, a half smile on his face. "Are you serious?"

"Yes, Baby. The doctor confirmed it today."

She bit her lip in an attempt to hold back her excitement.

"Oh my God." He said nearly in tears, "My baby! I'm so happy!" Dion said showing a side of himself that she had never seen before. He wasn't the scowling drug dealer that she had grown to fear. He wasn't the tyrant that everyone else perceived him as. He was just a regular guy that had just heard the most important news of his life. "This is for real right? Don't play with me Bridgette."

"Yes!" She confirmed, nodding, unable to hold back her smile.

"We're finally going to have a beautiful family." Dion said as he walked up to embrace her.

"We are a beautiful family, Dion." She smiled, leaning in for a kiss. "I love you."

"I love you too, baby!"

22

As the months passed, Bridgette and Michael remained in close communication. He wasn't initially going to call her again after she missed his wedding. However, being a man of his word, he made the call and she explained everything to him. She apologized for how harsh she had been to him over the past years. She told him about her pregnancy and how hard it was to conceive. She even vowed to remain in close communication and to be there when him and Courtney decided to have a baby. Michael, even though not enthused to hear about Bridgette's pregnancy, was supportive and promised to be the best friend he could, as well as provide whatever he could offer, support wise.

Bridgette had grown passed the point where she was going to let Dion control her. She had a life growing inside her now and she refused to allow her baby to be raised in any environment that was hostile. She made it clear to Dion that the verbal and physical abuse had to stop. Dion went from the angry, over obsessed psychopath that he was, to a more balanced and nurturing figure, at least to Bridgette.

Outside of their home he hadn't changed a bit. He was still the same hotheaded Dion ready to attack at any given notice. He was a ruthless drug dealer who wasn't about to let anything come between him and his money. But when it came to Bridgette, his only focus was protection. He had to protect his wife and he had to protect the seed that was growing in her stomach.

Michael and Courtney had grown a lot as well. Their relationship that was once in pieces had become stronger than ever. They were a happily married couple that fell deeper in love with each other each day. He had gone from the brooding man who would never let go of Bridgette, to the man who would do anything to make Courtney happy. He didn't let people push him around anymore. If he didn't like something he would be sure to address it and fix it. Michael had become a man.

When Bridgette entered her third trimester, Courtney started thinking about a baby of her own. Her and Michael had always joked around about it, but the thought of a newborn was one that she couldn't get out of her head.

"Michael," she said.

"I want to have a baby too."

He responded reluctantly, "Oh um… okay."

"Do you not want me to have your child, Mike?" she said, offended by his reluctance.

"Babe, you know that's not it. I'm just scared that's all. The thought of having created something so beautiful just… I don't know, intimidates me."

"I don't know why, you'd be the perfect dad."

"You think so?" He said trying to hide his smile.

"I know it."

"Then I would be honored if you had my baby. Let's just wait until we are ready financially."

"Agreed." Courtney smiled at the thought of having her own baby to take care of. And even though Michael's initial response wasn't the one she was looking for, she grew excited for the day when she could call herself a mother.

23

A tired and very pregnant Bridgette wobbled into the living room. She held the bottom of her stomach with her right hand. The baby was ready to escape and she was beyond ready to give birth to their beautiful child. She called to Dion who was sitting on the couch watching television.

"Baby! Um…" Bridgette hesitated. "It's time."

"For?" He responded uninterested.

"The baby is coming…Right now."

"Wow, yea…that's great!"

"Get up and let's go unless you're trying to deliver this baby yourself."

"Go where?"

"To the hospital, Dion. I just told you the baby was coming."

"I'm not going."

"What?" Bridgette said confused. "Why not?"

"I have some deliveries of my own to make soon…don't worry though, I'll be here when you get back."

"Dion, you're not funny. We need to go now!"

"I'm not tellin' jokes? I'm really not going."

"I need you right now!" Bridgette pleaded.

"You need? You know what you need? A nice house to live in! That nice ass car you drive. Money to buy all those petty things you *need*." Dion continued his angry rant. "That means I need to keep making this money… Driving a car isn't that hard. You're a big girl, I'm sure you'll figure it out."

"Fucking asshole!" Bridgette mumbled under her breath.

"What was that!?" He said, standing up in a fury.

"Nothing Dion!" Bridgette said, slamming the door behind her.

After all this time, it was hard for her to believe Dion hadn't changed. Everything that he had done those past months was just a front to get her through the pregnancy smoothly. Now he was back to his old self. Her emotions swarmed as she got in the car and began to drive. Tears flowed down her cheeks. Needing somebody, anybody to be with her, she removed her phone from her purse and called Michael.

"Hey Bridgette, what's going on?" He answered.

"Mike, I need you…It's time."

"Time? Wait… you're… the baby's coming?"

"Yes! I'm headed to the hospital now."

"Bridgette, are you okay?"

She hesitated. "Yeah, I'm okay."

Michael heard the distress in her voice. It worried him that something was wrong in her life. He didn't know if it was Dion or maybe something happened to the baby she wasn't telling. All he knew was his best friend was troubled and he needed to be there for her.

"Okay, Courtney and I will be there as soon as possible."

"Thank you, Mike."

"Yea, of course. I'm here anytime you need me."

They hung up and Michael ran to the bedroom still troubled by the way Bridgette sounded. .

"Courtney, Honey!" He called, receiving her attention. "Get dressed, we gotta go."

"Go? Where are we going?"

"To the hospital. Bridgette is having her baby."

"Well, why didn't you say so? C'mon!"

Bridgette remained torn apart from the way Dion acted. It was like he didn't love her anymore, like all that mattered was having a child. She began to wonder if after she had the baby if he would even still take care of her.

I need to stop thinking negative. She thought to herself. Her emotions were already high due to the pregnancy. *Maybe it's all just in my head. I know he still loves me so I need to get my mind together.*

Bridgette had phoned ahead to Dr. Daniels before leaving home so that he would be prepared to help bring her into the hospital. When she arrived at the emergency entrance, Michael and Courtney were at the curb with a wheel chair ready. Michael jogged to help her out the car, while Courtney wheeled the chair to her. They both observed Dion's absence, but it was Courtney who asked the question that was on both of their minds.

"Where's Dion?"

"Um," Bridgette hesitated, thinking of a cover story to tell. "He had to do something important, but…He promised to be here before the delivery."

"Ok then, let's just get you in there." Michael said.

Neither of them believed the lie that Bridgette told. Her tears were evidence that showed the real reason that he wasn't there; he just didn't want to be. Although it hurt Michael to see her like this, he accepted the fact that it really wasn't any of his business, at least not anymore.

With a combined effort they wheeled Bridgette into the emergency room and helped ready her for delivery.

24

Michael and Courtney stood by Bridgette's bedside waiting for Dr. Daniels. An hour had dragged along slowly, making Michael worry even more. He left the room and headed to the gift shop to find a present for when the baby arrived. As he wandered the empty halls, he thought, *I hope the baby's ok. Why else would she be crying when she pulled up?*

He walked into the low-lit gift shop and looked for a toy. There was a friendly older lady behind the counter counting money. "I'll be with you in a sec." she said.

"No rush I'm just browsing." Michael replied. He looked through the selection of toys and dolls, his eyes landing on a small plush teddy bear with a red tie. *This is perfect!* He grabbed it and took it to the register.

He made his way back to the room to find Bridgette and Courtney accompanied by Dr. Daniels. He concealed the bear behind his back. "How is she doing Doctor?" he asked.

"You must be Dion right?" The doctor replied with a smile on his face. Michael cringed at being called Dion.

"No Doctor, that's Mike. My best friend." Bridgette interrupted.

"Oh My apologies Mike. Bridgette and the baby are doing fine. She should be going into labor soon."

"Ok great thanks Doctor!" Michael responded. *I guess I was just worrying for nothing.* He thought, returning his attention to Bridgette.

"Bridgette, guess what I have?" He said smiling with anticipation.

"What did you buy, my love?" Courtney questioned.

"It's a bear for the baby!"

The ladies smiled warmly as Bridgette accepted the gift.

"Mike you didn't have to—"

"Yes, I did." He quickly interrupted. "The baby deserves a warm welcome. Besides, it's from both of us."

"Well, thank you."

"It's no problem, really." Courtney said.

"No, seriously…I thank you two for coming on such short notice.

"Are you kidding? We wouldn't miss the birth of your first child…I mean, we're practically the aunt and uncle."

Bridgette giggled at Courtney's response. "That is true."

"So how far are we? I mean you. Um, how close are you to delivering?" Michael stammered nervously.

The ladies loved watching how nervous Michael was. Although, all he had to do was wait, he clearly believed there was so much more he should do. Courtney stared at him with love in her eyes thinking back to their conversation about their first child. *He's gonna be a great dad!* She thought.

"Dr. Daniels said it shouldn't be long from now til' I go into labor. I'm just really ready for it to be over. All I keep thinking about is how much pain I'm gonna be in."

"Woman to woman," Courtney began with a smile. "You'll be fine. God made us to endure the pain."

"You're right,"

Bridgette was grateful to have Courtney there; she needed a woman around that she could relate to. She realized that Courtney was the closest thing to having a real girlfriend these days even though they weren't close. Liz and Becca hadn't spoken to her much since her and Dion got married.

"I may have went crazy if it were just Mike and I..."
Bridgette said that with sarcasm.

"I am standing right here, you know?" Michael defended.

"We see you honey," Courtney joked as the ladies laughed
amongst themselves.

"Is Dion gonna be here soon?" Courtney repeated her
question from earlier. She had let Bridgette shy away from
answering before but now she was genuinely curious. Michael
had thought about the same thing since she got to the hospital,
but he thought it best to leave it alone.

"He had to work." Bridgette replied.

Yeah, right. Michael thought in rage. He knew Dion didn't
have a traditional job. He was a drug dealer. There was no set
schedule for him. He came and went as he pleased.

"Really? You would think they would let him off for
something as big as this." Courtney questioned.

"Yeah, you would think?" Bridgette replied.

He's really not gonna come. Bridgette thought,
disappointed. *He's seriously gonna make me do this alone.*
Dion still hadn't arrived and each passing minute was a
minute closer to her going into labor.

Before any more questions were asked, Dr. Daniels arrived.

"Okay Bridgette. It looks like the time is almost here. How are you feeling?"

"I'm so nervous!" It was like all of the emotions she'd felt before Courtney calmed her down were rushing through her system again.

"It's your first time having a baby, so naturally you should feel like this, but rest assured there is nothing to be nervous about. We'll walk you through the whole process and I'll be with you every step of the way."

Bridgette nodded.

"Did you want either of your friends to accompany you in the Delivery Room?"

"I'll do it!" Michael jumped at the chance. Courtney looked at him in disbelief that he would even consider something like that. She liked Bridgette but there was no way she would allow Michael out of her sight when Bridgette was around.

"No, that's fine. I don't think Dion would like it if he showed and one of you were in there with me."

Michael knew it was directed specifically toward him, but he understood nonetheless.

"But thanks anyway." Bridgette said smiling.

"Very well then. I think we should get you prepped so you can soon meet your baby. What do you think?" The doctor asked while washing his hands.

Bridgette took a few deep breaths and as important as this moment and the baby were to her; the thought at the front of her mind was knowing Dion was going to miss the birth of his child.

"I think I'm ready now."

"If you change your mind and decide you need someone in there with you," Courtney started. "I'll gladly come to be with you so you're not alone. We'll be in the waiting room. All you have to do is let the doctor or a nurse know, okay?"

Bridgette nodded and smiled.

"Good luck." Courtney finished.

A million questions raced through Michael's head. He wanted to remind Bridgette of how horrible Dion was for not showing up. He wanted to let her know that she needed to dump him as soon as this was over. But Michael knew that none of his concerns about Dion held importance at that moment. The only thing that mattered is that Bridgette was comfortable. "I'm so excited for you Bridgette!" He offered.

With that, Michael gave her a hug, hoping the familiarity of his love would comfort her during her birth giving. He looked her in the eyes and smiled. *Nothing gonna ruin this*, he thought as he and Courtney began their walk to the waiting room.

25

The sun peeked in through the window of the waiting room. Courtney squinted her eyes and stretched as she looked to Michael who was still asleep in his chair. The clock read 8:15; it had been nearly 10 hours since they last saw Bridgette. Courtney laid her head on Michael's shoulder and dozed back off.

They had spent the entire night side by side in each other's arms. Their two chairs were separated by plastic armrests, which made sleeping nearly impossible. Dr. Daniels entered the waiting room and saw them peacefully together. He tapped Michael on the shoulder and cleared his throat before speaking.

"Excuse me, Sir." He said, startling Michael from his sleep. "You can see Bridgette and the baby now."

"It's over? The baby is here?" Michael said attempting to fully wake up.

"Yes. The delivery was successful." The doctor smiled.

"Courtney, wake up!" Michael urged, gently tapping her on the shoulder. "Bridgette is awake, the baby is born...C'mon, let's go see them."

Courtney yawned and nodded as she rose from her slumber.

"Just so you know," Dr. Daniels started. "Bridgette is still tired, but she requested to see the two of you before she had to get more rest."

"Thank you, Doctor."

The two of them rushed to see the new addition.

26

The doctor entered Bridgette's room, Courtney and Michael closely behind him. A tired and puffy-eyed Bridgette lay in her bed, baby in hand. She looked beautiful, even with her wildly untamed hair, and her unfashionable hospital gown. It was definitely the distinct glow of a first time mother holding her newborn child. She looked up to the trio and offered a welcoming smile.

"How are you feeling?" Michael asked.

Bridgette didn't answer him. Her attention was fully on her baby. She gently rubbed his nearly bald head. He stretched his small arms and began to fuss. His messy cry was like music to her.

"I love you so much." She whispered to her son, calming him.

"Bridgette, how—"

"I heard you the first time Mike." She smiled. "And I'm fine..." Her voice was hoarse. She briefly looked up at her audience but quickly returned her attention to the baby.

"You look Radiant." Courtney noticed.

"That's how I feel." Tears gathered in Bridgette's eyes. Anytime she had spoken about the baby she would cry. This was a repeating pattern. "I was in labor for thirty hours. All of it was very painful...and yet all of it was worth it to feel the joy I have in my heart."

Tears came again.

"It was actually nine hours," Dr. Daniels inputted smiling, as happy as the others.

Bridgette blushed. "Thank you again, Doctor! For everything."

"That's what I'm here for... Just let me know if you need anything else. By the way, I have also had the nurse contact your husband for you as requested." She nodded. "Now, if you will excuse me, I need to finish up some paperwork before I leave. Congratulations again!"

The doctor exited the room while Michael and Courtney examined the baby.

"Have you already named him?" Michael asked.

Bridgette nodded. "Dion," Michael rolled his eyes. "Dion Allen Ross…Named after his father."

Of course. Michael thought. *I don't know why I even asked.*

"Oh, Okay…That's a great name." He said faking a smile.

Michael couldn't believe the amount of resentment he still had in his heart toward Dion. However, he ignored it all because today was the celebration of new life. At this moment it was all about Bridgette and her baby.

"Can I hold him?"

"Sorry, Mike." Bridgette said with sorrow on her face. She felt bad because she didn't mind Michael holding Baby Dion. "I wanted Dion to be the first person to hold him other than myself. You know how he is."

"Yea, of course. Totally understandable." Michael smiled awkwardly. He knew exactly how Dion would react. He knew that for Dion, his ego was more important than anything else.

"I still can't believe it," Michael started, trying to change the subject. "It feels like just yesterday we were little kids in school, running around with basically no worries, and now look at you." He smiled, proudly at Bridgette. "All grown up and starting your family."

"Thank you, Mike. I really appreciate how you've always been there for me."

Bridgette was very emotional. She wasn't sure what the reasoning for it was, but it wasn't a bad thing. Everything she felt was real, for the first time in a long time. She was deeply in love with the life she had created.

"Michael, Courtney. I know this request I'm going to make may sound strange, but hear me out." They nodded. "I would like you both to retain guardianship of Baby Dion. Like, if anything were to ever happen to us, Heaven forbid." She quickly added. "You could take care of him."

"Bridgette, nothing is going to happen to you two."

"Mike, I know. It would just make me feel better."

"Well," Michael hesitated. "I would have to go over it with Courtney, but if she's okay with it…" His attention directed toward his wife and their eyes met.

"I would be honored, Bridgette. Thank you." Courtney was very grateful and humbled that Bridgette trusted them enough to take guardianship. "Now can we please talk about something else? Like this beautiful baby right here?"

"Yes, we can. Just know that I'm really thankful for you guys."

Michael and Courtney smiled. The room filled with love as they stared in awe at the beautiful baby boy. The moment was wonderful until Dion entered the room. He walked passed everyone, ignoring their presence and approached Bridgette with a giddy look smeared on his face.

"Oh my God!" He began. "That's me? That's my son?"

"Yes baby, it is!"

"Did you already name him?"

I did." She smiled. "I would like you to meet Dion Allen Ross, the second."

"He's beautiful! Just like his mama." They shared a smile. "I love you Bridgette!"

"I love you too."

Michael and Courtney watched and smiled while the new parents shared time together. They looked happy for the first time in a long time.

27

After nine months, life with a baby around was everything Bridgette and Dion expected it to be, different. They were finally happy and all the drama they were involved with over the last years was irrelevant. The headaches of trying to get pregnant were over and Dion was more than happy to take responsibility as a proud father.

Bridgette was enjoying life with her new family. She couldn't stop showing her son off to friends and relatives. She took pictures at every given opportunity. She posted them online for everyone to see her beautiful family. Her favorite thing to see now was the sight of Dion being a father to his son. She finally had the life she longed for.

The thought of having a son was incredible to Dion. He took pride in the fact that he had created something so perfect. He bragged daily about how good looking, smart and overall amazing his baby was. He cut down his drinking and would never smoke near the baby. His mental state became steadier. When he and Bridgette would fight all she had to do was mention the baby and it would silence Dion almost instantly. In fact the only problem Dion ever saw in the baby was its skin color. Dion was dark-skinned and assumed the baby would be as well. He constantly questioned when Baby Dion would gain his color but at this point those questions remained unanswered.

28

Dion entered the living room to find Bridgette readying herself and the baby to go to the store. He walked up to Baby Dion's crib and hovered over, looking into his son's eyes as he lay there. He smiled, examining the tiny child who grinned back, happy to see his father. Baby Dion had grown a full head of curly hair and already had his first tooth. He was eating solid foods and was extremely playful. Dion picked up his son by the torso and held him high in the air.

"Why hasn't it gotten dark?" He asked Bridgette.

"What do you mean?"

Bridgette waked over to take a look at what Dion was referring to. She realized he was referring to their son, which irritated her.

"*He*, hasn't gotten dark because sometimes it takes longer for a baby to get their color. In rare occasions, the baby won't even get color."

"My son should be darker than this."

"Well don't forget we are a mixed couple, Dion."

"I guess so," Dion didn't like what he was seeing, what he was feeling about his son. The skin, the hair color, the eyes. Something wasn't adding up. He had a gut feeling that something wasn't right.

"It just seems weird." He finally finished.

"Dion, can't you just appreciate that we have a happy, healthy little boy?" She stressed. "Our son needs us to be happy and to be there for him, always. Okay? It shouldn't matter if he looks different from us, that's our son."

"Yeah," He nodded. His suspicion was still rising to the forefront of his mind. "You're right." Dion felt there was no reason to get into it with Bridgette, so he dropped the subject, for now. "Hey, but go ahead and run to the store. I'll watch the baby."

"Really?"

"Yea...I think we need some father son time."

"Wow!" Bridgette smiled, almost in disbelief. It wasn't often that she got to go shopping by herself. "Ok, it's so much harder to buy food with a baby trying to grab everything in sight." She leaned in and gave both Dion's a kiss before exiting the house. "See you guys in a bit."

Dion returned his attention to the baby.

Something's not right. He thought to himself.

Dion hurriedly picked up his phone and called Brad.

"Ay Brad," Dion started. "Remember when that girl said you knocked her up?"

"Yeah, what about it?"

"How long did the paternity test take?"

"If you pay for it to be rushed then you could have the results paper in your hand the next day, wait..." Brad paused as a thought came to his mind. "Don't tell me you knocked some random bitch up. I told you a million times about messing with them—"

"Shut up and tell me the address of the place." Dion snarled.

"It's on 5th and Juniper St. it's some doctor's office where babies get their shots and all that. I can't remember what it's called"

"Fa sho, thanks." Dion hung up the phone and gazed at his son.

He hated being lied to. He knew Bridgette wouldn't ever cheat on him, but still he had to make sure that Baby Dion was indeed Baby Dion.

"C'mon *son*," He said with much uncertainty. "Let's take a ride."

He placed the baby in the car seat and left the house hurriedly. He needed to get the paternity test before Bridgette got home.

Later that night, the question still remained. Dion wasn't able to sleep. He glanced over at Bridgette who slept comfortably beside him. He propped himself upright and slid his legs to the side until his feet touched the carpet beneath. He sat at the edge of the bed for a couple of minutes before standing and walking to the baby's crib in the next room.

He's gotta be my son. His mind wandered.

Dion studied the baby intently, taking careful caution not to wake him. *He kinda has my nose.* Dion thought trying to convince himself that he was over reacting. *He's got his mom's mouth and eyes.* The longer he observed baby Dion, the more the question of Bridgette's infidelity grew. He had to know the truth.

"You look like your mom," He whispered. "But are you my son?"

29

The next morning, Dion sat on the couch, awaiting the mailman to bring the envelope he'd been stressing about all night. Bridgette was cleaning the house oblivious to what Dion was doing. At a point, she noticed the way Dion's eyes consistently carried toward the window.

"What are you doing?" She asked curiously.

"Just waiting for the mail to come."

"Expecting a package?"

"Yeah, something like that."

"Oh, what did you order?"

"What are you Customs now? Damn."

"Sorry Dion, geez."

Bridgette was used to Dion snapping at her for asking a lot of questions. She figured it was nothing out of the ordinary. As for Dion, his only focus was finding out the answer to his burning question. He knew the baby had to be his. He was sure that the results would prove him to be the father. But while he was waiting he couldn't do or say anything to make

Bridgette stay home. He had to play nice until he knew the truth.

"Baby, I'm just looking for the mail." He said, pretending to be sweet.

"Mmhmm…I'm going to Yoga. I'll be back at 6, okay?"

"Yea."

The mailman finally drove up to their mailbox and placed their mail within. As the truck drove off he rushed outside. He quickly searched through the mail until he found the letter and concealed it into his pocket.

"Well?" Bridgette's curiosity was peaking.

"Well what?" Dion deflected; irritated at the fact she was still there.

"Did you get your mystery package?"

Dion took a second to think.

"Nah," He lied guiltlessly. "It didn't come in."

"Did I get anything?"

He handed her the stack of mail, and anxiously watched her sift through the pile.

"Aren't you supposed to be leaving? Those curves won't carve themselves."

Bridgette looked at Dion sideways, intrigued of his sudden hostility toward her the last couple of days. She left it alone as she figured something else had been on his mind. "Yea, I know..." She smiled. "I'm leaving right now, okay? Try and keep it down, the baby is sleeping."

Dion nodded. As soon as she left he ripped open the envelope containing the results. As his eyes skimmed through the words, his mind wandered to the worst places, not knowing what to expect. In about a minute he discovered the answer he had been waiting for. The message read:

Through sixteen matching procedures to include hair follicle, blood and saliva glands, He read to himself, just until thoughts began to speak from his mouth "It can be stated with a 99.9% accuracy, that Dion Allen Ross is **NOT** the Father of Dion Allen Ross Jr."

Dion read exactly what he feared deep down he would. He had convinced himself that all though he cheated all the time and had little regard for their relationship, Bridgette would always remain faithful. It wasn't until this moment that he realized how wrong he was.

"She cheated—"

He wasn't able to finish a sentence with the feeling of his heart being tugged at and then ripped out of his chest. Dion cried. For the first time in a long time, Dion cried. He'd never expected this behavior from the woman he loved. Bridgette had always been a faithful woman, so for her to go behind his back and have a baby by another man broke him down.

He paced about the living room in a rage. His head swarmed with malicious ideas of how he could get his revenge on the promiscuous Bridgette. *She thinks she can cheat on me? I got her! All the shit I've done for her. The nice ass shit I've bought her and she thinks she can go sleep around.* Anger built in his stomach, tears of rage now flowing down his cheeks. *I'm the reason this bitch even has a life. But she won't have one for long.*

He rushed to the coffee table where he had left his phone and called Brad.

"Yo, Dion!" Brad greeted. "So did you get your results?"

"Never mind all that!"

It was apparent to Brad that Dion had gotten some bad news, but he didn't ask what because he knew Dion would've snapped on him.

"Meet me at the warehouse on 13th at eight. I'm bringing company!"

Without another word said, Dion hung up the phone. Immediately after he called his mother for a favor.

"Hey Mom," Dion said getting right to the point. "Could you watch the baby tonight? B and I are having a date night."

She happily agreed as Dion rushed her off the phone. There was only one more call for him to make at this point and it was to Bridgette. He took a moment to gather his thoughts. He wanted to scream at her but he knew that if she got wind of his newfound knowledge, there would be no way she would go anywhere with him. Unable to calm himself down enough to speak to her, he sent a text message instead.

*Come straight home after yoga…*the text started, *we're going out, so I need you to wear something nice. Tonight's gonna be unforgettable.*

He had the night all setup. Everything would go as planned as long as he kept his cool. All he needed to do now was wait until 8 o'clock and the show could begin.

30

Bridgette arrived home to an empty house. A note was on the coffee table saying.

Droppin' the baby off at Mom's be ready when I get back.
–Dion

She hurried to her closet to pick out what she would wear for the evening, hopped in the shower and got ready. She wore a form-fitting black dress that reached right above her knee, black stiletto heels, and a pair of diamond earrings to match her wedding ring. All she had left to do was finish her make-up. Dion walked into the house and called for her. "Bridgette! Let's go."

"One second baby," she replied. "Just finishing my make-up."

How dare you call me baby? I'm not you're fucking baby. He thought, growing more impatient by the second.

"You can do that in the car. I don't wanna be late." He barked, ready to get the night over with. His words alarmed Bridgette, but a smile rose to her face. They hadn't gone out on a date night in a long time. "Okay Dion, here I come."

They traveled down the road in silence. Dion drove while Bridgette painted her face with make-up using the sun-visor mirror. Attempting to break the silence Bridgette asked, "So are you going to tell me where we're going?"

The sound of her voice was the last thing he wanted to hear. For him the silence was a way to contain his anger. But as the silence had been interrupted, there wasn't anything to keep him from letting go. He snapped. He slapped her across the face, her makeup compact spilling over her dress. A red hand print bruise immediately showed as he struck her again this time with his fist closed.

"You think you can cheat on me, bitch?"

"What are you talking about!?" she cried.

She held the side of her face tightly. Dumbfounded by the entire event.

"You know what I'm talking about."

"I don't, I swear."

"You trifling bitch!"

He reached in his jacket pocket. She flinched thinking he was going to reveal a weapon. Instead he handed her the white folded paper containing the results for the paternity test. "What is this Dion?"

"Read it!" He growled, speaking through his teeth.

As she read the horrifying results of the test, her eyes filled with tears. Dion was about to discover a secret that she intended to take with her to the grave. "Dion, it's not what you think. I never cheated on you, I swear."

"Don't fucking lie to me!" He said, hitting her two more times.

There was no letting it go for him.

"Just listen!" she pleaded. He sat in silence as she explained. "I was so afraid, Dion. I heard you say you were going to kill me if I didn't get pregnant and I knew you would. I tried so many things to make myself more fertile, I tried to make sure I would conceive, but nothing worked. Then I spoke to the doctor and told him about my problem, that's when he made another suggestion. He told me about this procedure that helps couples that couldn't have kids on their own. He told me it was starting to become more and more popular; it's called Artificial Insemination. He said that you get sperm from a male donor and they force a pregnancy..."

The livid Dion quietly continued to listen to her farfetched story.

"I knew how much you wanted to be a father, Dion...I did it for us!"

"You lying, bitch!" Dion's rage had been fueled even more after hearing a story so ridiculous. "You're gonna fucking lie to me? Do you think I'm fucking stupid? Did you think I wouldn't find out?" He interrogated her as she begged for understanding.

"Dion I—"

"Shut the hell up!" He screamed, "I'm going to fucking kill you."

With those last words, Dion released the steering wheel and wrapped his hands around Bridgette's throat. She fought for air, but his hold was too tight. The car swerved as they neared the bridge. Bridgette gazed out the front view window and realized the danger he had just put them in by letting go of the steering wheel. She reached her left hand out to try to stabilize the car and grabbed the wheel. But in her attempt, she over corrected the tires, heading them for the right railing of the bridge. Her eyes widened, while Dion's attention left her and back to the road.

He grabbed hold of the wheel and turned the car hard left to avoid the railing they were now heading for, but it wouldn't help much. The car's wheels slid across the ground sideways, the smell of burnt rubber stained the air. He tried frantically to regain control, maneuvering the wheel to the left and right, but sadly it wouldn't be enough. The speeding car barreled through the side railing of the bridge stopping for only a split second before plummeting in the underlying river. Neither Bridgette nor Dion would survive.

31

"And this was the graphic scene around 3a.m. as local firefighters frantically attempted to save the passengers of the sports utility vehicle that drove over the railing and into the ravine..." The news anchor reported. Courtney watched intently as they played footage of a black vehicle being lifted from the river by crane.

"...No one knows the cause of the accident, but the LA Coroner's office has confirmed that the two bodies found within the vehicle were Mr. and Mrs. Dion Allen Ross. Sadly neither of the victims survived..."

As the pictures of the victims flashed on the TV screen, a cold chill ran down Courtney's spine. Questions and tears immediately followed. *What about the baby? Was he in the car too?* And then she had a horrifying realization. *It's gonna DESTROY Mike!* The news reporter continued.

"...Witnesses say that the car swerved back and forth across the asphalt until it finally collided with the right side of bridge's railing that you can see here. The cause of this tragic event is still under investigation."

Courtney sat paralyzed with emotion. She was about to have to do the hardest thing she has ever done. She had to devastate the man she loved by telling him that his best friend in the entire world was gone. She shuffled her hand across the couch, searching for her phone. She dialed Michael's work. "Hi," she said struggling to speak. "Could you have Michael Smith come home, it's urgent. Please tell him to hurry…this is his wife."

Time stood still for Courtney as she racked her brain to figure out the way to break the news to Michael. All she could hope was that he didn't go back into the depressed state that they had fought so hard to free him from. She feared that he would hear the news somehow or get a call from someone and he wouldn't even be able to make it home safely. Finally after about 20 minutes, she heard the cylinder of the deadbolt lock turn. Michael was home.

He walked in the house clueless as to what was going on. He spotted a broken Courtney crying on the couch. She ran to him and hugged him tightly, refusing to let go.

"What's wrong?" Michael pleaded but Courtney couldn't offer an answer. "It's okay Courtney. I'm sure everything is going to be fine." Michael assured. She brought him to the couch and sat him down. She turned on the television and went to the DVR recording of what she had been watching. And with a heavy heart, she played the news report back for him to watch.

Michael sat frozen in shock after witnessing the tragedy. He picked up the remote and replayed the clip over and over. He wasn't sure if he was dreaming or it was some cruel joke, but he refused to believe it was true. And after about the 5th time watching it, Michael broke down. He screamed "Bridgette! No!" Tears flowed freely down his face and his body began to shake. Courtney grabbed him and held him close. He had never felt as powerless as he did in that moment. His best friend was gone. A woman he loved and cared for his entire life, gone in an instant.

Courtney continued to hold Michael for the next hour as he cried uncontrollably. She wasn't sure if she was more saddened by the loss of Bridgette or to see her husband devastated like this. But she would do all she could to comfort him and help him get through it.

He looked to the sky. *How could they be gone?* He questioned. *God, why did this have to happen? You just blessed them with a baby of their own and then just like that the baby's parents were taken away. I don't understand.*

There was no answer for Michael; all that he could do was cry. For the next few days this was a repeating cycle. Courtney stood by his side, mourning with him. Her support was the only thing that kept him from falling back into the darkness of depression that he once suffered from.

32

The day both Michael and Courtney had dreaded arrived. Darkness hovered over the heads of the couple as they silently readied themselves for the mourning of two people, one whom they both considered to be a significant part of their lives. "I love you Michael." Courtney said attaching the clasp on her necklace.

Michael stood in front of the mirror wearing his all black ensemble. He gripped his tie tightly in his hands after tying it in an Eldredge knot. The pain was so heavy in his heart that he felt as if he was the one who had died and that he was preparing for his own services. "I love you too!" He said solemnly.

Michael wasn't himself. He began remembering the night when he attempted to take his own life. *Is this how Bridgette and Courtney would have felt?* He asked himself. *Would it have been worst?*

The questions continued to flood his mind as he stroked down on his tie and took a couple of deep breaths.

"Are you ready to go?" Courtney asked, concerned.

Michael nodded once more. "Yeah, I think so."

When they arrived at the funeral parlor, Michael was barely able to contain himself. He saw some recognizable faces of people they went to school with. Liz and Becca sat together in a pew waiting for the services to start. Dion's mother and other family members walked past the closed caskets crying, barely able to stand. A large floral reef sat atop one of the caskets, inside it a picture of Bridgette and Dion at their wedding.

Finally Michael spotted Bridgette's mother sitting with her father and some other family members he didn't recognize. He walked up to her and hugged her tight. This was the first time she had seen him since her daughter's wedding. He introduced Courtney and after a few words of catching up, he made his way towards the caskets.

How would he feel when he walked by? Knowing his best friend was lying in that wooden box, truly lifeless. Knowing she would never return by his side? The thought alone petrified him, but he knew he had to show his last respects.

It was his and Courtney's turn to pass by the caskets. Michael didn't want to think about how he'd react if his wife wasn't by his side. Deep in his heart, Michael was relieved that the last image he would keep of Bridgette would be her smiling and full of life. He and Courtney paused at the side of Bridgette's coffin and said a prayer.

As they walked away, Michael wiped his face with his handkerchief. An usher approached them and pointed out their seats. The services began and Michael did his best to contain his emotions. As the reverend delivered the eulogy, Courtney held Michael's hand in a constant show of support. Family and friends of the departed shared memories of good times. Finally, Bridgette's mother came up and said her peace. Before stepping down, she requested that Michael say something as well.

He hated speaking in front of crowds. But he walked to the podium and gazed out to the congregation. "Bridgette was..." He tried to speak but no words came out. Just a few tears and unspoken thoughts. He apologized and returned to his seat.

After the ceremony, family and friends gathered at the repast; but Michael and Courtney decided to skip it all together. The funeral had left the both of them exhausted. The said their goodbye's and left.

While walking toward their car, Michael and Courtney were approached by a man in a black suit.

"Mr. and Mrs. Michael Smith?" The mystery man asked cautiously.

"Yes, and you are?" Michael responded.

"Hi, my name is Joseph Vero. Would it be alright if I spoke with the two of you, privately?"

"Yeah," Michael said reluctantly. "That's fine."

"Alright then, right this way." Michael and Courtney followed Mr. Vero to a small room in the church.

"Please, sit."

They did as invited and prepared themselves to listen. "May I know what this is about?" Michael demanded.

"I know this is an incredibly difficult time for the both of you and I would like to offer my deepest and most sincere condolences for your loss."

"Thank you." The couple said in unison.

"But it is very important that I talk to you about Mr. and Mrs. Ross." Mr. Vero continued.

"Are you a detective or something?" Courtney asked.

"Oh, Heavens no…I'm a case worker. I was given your file this morning…"

"File?" Michael interrupted sharing a confused look with Courtney.

"Yes." Mr. Vero nodded as he pulled a folder from his suitcase. "When Mrs. Ross had her baby, Dion Allen Ross Jr., the two of you signed guardianship papers that in the event of Mr. and Mrs. Ross not being able to take care of their child you would have the first option to adopt. Do you remember signing these papers?

The couple nodded.

"I know that this is a very big decision for the both of you to make under these circumstances, however, if you are not sure at this moment then we will be forced to begin processing Dion Allen Ross Jr. immediately."

"What do you mean processing?" Michael questioned.

"For adoption." Mr. Vero replied. "Luckily though, he's very young and we should be able to find him a foster family fairly easily. It's common for families to request children under a year."

"Um…" Michael hesitated… "May I have a moment to speak to my wife?"

"Certainly."

"What do—?"

"Let's do it!" Courtney interrupted, already knowing her position on the matter.

"Really?"

"Yeah," She reassured. "There's no point of that beautiful baby going through the foster care system, and besides, we could use some practice until we have children of our own."

"I love you so much." He smiled.

Michael was grateful that he and his wife were on the same page with the adoption. It meant the world to him to have a chance to take care of someone who Bridgette cared for so much. He turned to Mr. Vero, who'd already heard Courtney's response and gave him their answer.

"We'll do it!"

"Great, now if the two of you will just sign on the line, I will take these papers over to your case worker. They will provide you the rest of the documentation you will need to fill out before you can pick up Dion Allen Ross Jr. I would like to thank you both for your time once again, and you should know that you've done a great thing going through with the adoption."

Michael and Courtney felt good about their decision together, not just because they would be giving a child a home, but also because they were given a chance to make a real difference in Baby Dion's life.

"Thank you, Mr. Vero," Michael said as he reached out to shake his hand. "I know I speak for my wife, as well as for myself, when I say we're grateful you came to us today."

"You're very welcome, God bless the both of you."

33

Michael and Courtney were now the legal guardians of baby Dion and now all that was left for them to do was to fill out the necessary papers requesting the baby's medical records. Courtney held their new son in her arms while Michael handed the clipboard and completed paperwork to the clerk sitting behind the counter at the doctor's office. The clerk keyed in the information provided into the computer.

"Okay, it looks like his shot records are up to date. You will need to bring him in at twelve months for his Hepatitis A, HIB, MMR, PCV and Chickenpox shots." The clerk handed Michael a piece of paper. "And here is a list of his known allergies and…" The clerk paused.

"Is everything Okay?" Courtney asked, worried by the clerk's reaction.

The clerk read the paper again just to verify what was seen.

"What is it?" Michael demanded, alarmed as well.

"Well, it shows here that there was a paternity test issued two days before the accident."

"A paternity test?" Courtney said. "Why would they need a test to—?" Her gaze now fixed on Michael. "Can I see that paper?"

The clerk handed Courtney the paper and she and Michael read it together.

*Through sixteen matching procedures to include hair follicle, blood and saliva glands, it can be stated with a 99.9% accuracy, that Dion Allen Ross is **NOT** the Father of Dion Allen Ross Jr.*

"Not possible," Michael shook his head in disbelief. "She would never cheat on anyone, not even someone as horrible as Dion." He defended. Michael was assured the paternity test was mistaken. "I know her better than that."

"Michael, please don't tell me..." Courtney said to him in disgust. She had already drawn up many conclusions in her mind. "Is that why you couldn't let her go? Were you cheating on me with her this entire time?"

Courtney was angry, but because she didn't know the whole truth, she did her best to control herself.

"Baby, I've never touched her!" Michael said sincerely. "I've never been with anyone except for you."

"Then take a paternity test."

Michael looked at Courtney is disbelief. How could she not trust him after all they had been through?

"Okay, I will. I'll take the test because there is no way this baby is mine."

Shortly after, a paternity test was issued. They swabbed baby Dion's mouth, took blood, and hair follicles. They did the same with Michael. They paid for the expedited results to be available the next day. And with many unanswered questions the family went home and waited.

34

A small vase hurled through the air, leaving Courtney's hand, barely missing Michael before it shattered against the wall. Michael put his hands up in defense attempting to shield himself from her rage. The sound of baby Dion crying could be heard in the background. The angry wife had been screaming at the top of her lungs at her confused husband, scaring not only the baby, but also Michael a little as well. His cell phone rang during the heated moment but he ignored the call.

"I swear to God! I don't know how it happened, but this is not my son." Michael pleaded.

"I know how it happened! You slept with her and now you don't have the grapes to admit it...was it good Mike, huh? Was it worth it!?"

She grabbed a picture frame from the mantle and threw it at him. This time he had to duck to avoid contact.

"Baby, stop please listen to me!" His hands still held up between them. The exhausted Courtney plopped down on the couch. "What could you possibly have to say to me, Michael?"

His phone rang again and this time he answered it, seeing that their fight had simmered, slightly.

"Mike, brotha, what's up?" It was his friend Sergio.

"Hey man, right now is really not a good time."

"That's okay, I just need to ask a quick favor."

"What is it?"

"I need to borrow fifty bucks."

"Man, couldn't it wait? I'm in the middle of something serious."

"Hey, you're the one who answered the phone, but you know I wouldn't ask if it weren't important."

Courtney listened intently to what Michael was saying, hoping to figure out who he was talking to.

"Dude I gotta go. Why don't you just go to the clinic like we used too?"

"Oh yeah, the clinic." Sergio smiled on his end. "We used to love that place! Thanks bro."

No sooner than they hung up the phone, Courtney shot up off the couch.

"The Clinic huh? Is that where you got tested for all your whores? Huh Mike? Is that where you visited twice a week to check your venereal diseases?"

Michael stared at Courtney in awe. He had never seen her lose her patience. Even when they would fight she would never say things to intentionally hurt him. *Why wouldn't she listen to reason? How come she wouldn't believe him when he was telling her the truth?* He thought.

"It's a sperm bank, Courtney. I only went there to get money when I lost my job. Sergio told me about that place so I didn't lose my apartment too."

Michael did his best to keep calm, as he explained to the non-believing Courtney.

"I already told you I hit rock bottom after you left me. You know that. I had no way to stay afloat. What else was I gonna do?"

"You're a liar Mike! You're lying to me! How come you can't just admit that you got a married woman pregnant?"

Courtney turned and attempted to walk away, but Michael grabbed her arm and made her listen to him.

"Why won't you believe me?" Michael raised his voice. "I have been nothing but faithful to you since the moment we got together."

"You wanted to be with her!"

"Yea, okay, I did, but that was before and I made peace with those demons. I wanted to be with Bridgette, I wanted to marry her, and I wanted her to have my child. But what you can't seem to see is that I chose you. I left her in my past because you loved me and I loved you and there was no one else in the world I wanted to be with after I saw where I was supposed to be."

"Makes sense, and then you go and get her pregnant." Courtney said facetiously

"Dion couldn't even get her pregnant!" He rebutted.

"What did you just say?" She asked angrily.

Michael sighed and explained. "Her and Dion tried for months to get pregnant but it wouldn't work. She did fertility treatments and everything but she got nowhere. She said the doctor was trying some experimental procedures and finally she…" He stopped mid-sentence.

"She what?" Courtney asked intrigued by the story.

Michael gasped, "No fucking Way!" He pulled out his cell phone and called information. "Can you get me Dr. Daniel's office?"

"What are you do—?" Courtney began, but her voice trailed off when Michael put his finger up, signaling her to wait.

"Hi, I need to speak with Dr. Daniels. Is he in?"

"One second please." The operator said.

After a few moments he answered. "Dr. Daniels speaking."

"Dr. Daniels, its Michael Smith."

"Oh, hey Michael. What can I do for you?"

"Is it a bad time for me to come speak with you?

"No, not if you can be here within the next twenty minutes."

Michael was relieved. "Thank you, I'll be there in five."

Michael didn't take the time to tell Courtney what he was up to. He needed to know if what he was thinking was correct. He hurried out of the door, quickly closing it behind him leaving Courtney with the baby, and clearly confused.

35

Michael pulled up to emergency parking and jumped out of his car. He ran through the glass sliding double doors and past the receptionist. He remembered where Dr. Daniel's office was from when Bridgette delivered so getting there was not a problem.

"Dr. Daniels!" Michael said, fighting to catch his breath as he entered the office.

"Awe, you made it," He looked at the clock. "Wow and in less than ten minutes." Michael smiled slightly but only nodded, as he had to finish catching his breath. "So what seems to be the problem?"

"I need to know about Bridgette's baby."

"Oh, was there a problem with the guardianship paperwork?"

"No, not that. I needed to know if the conception was normal."

"If that's what you drove here for then I'm sorry, Mike. I'm not able to give you that kind of information. It violates my Hippocratic oath."

"Dr. Daniels, you don't understand." He paused. "I have reason to believe that the baby is mine."

"I'm sorry, Michael. I can't."

"Doctor, I have a right to know and so does my wife. Courtney is already upset with me and I don't want us not knowing leading us to getting a divorce. That wouldn't be good for the baby."

Dr. Daniels could see that Michael needed to know. If this were a regular situation, he would've held his position firmly. However, seeing Michael in front of him practically begging led him to make his decision.

"Michael close the door and have a seat."

Michael did as instructed and sat down in front of the doctor's desk.

Now I can't say much and whatever I do say is strictly off the record."

"Thank you!"

Dr. Daniels nodded. "Bridgette and her husband, Dion, were having some difficulties conceiving. She tried many different methods, but ultimately she needed artificial insemination. That is the method of which impregnated her."

"Really?" Michael was relieved to hear the news. "Can you hold on for just one second?"

Dr. Daniels nodded as Michael called Courtney.

"Michael, what is going on?" She demanded, her voice riddled with anger and confusion.

"Courtney, baby...I need you to come to the hospital right now."

"Mike I told you I'm done!"

"If you come right now I'll never ask you for anything else. And if you want, I'll be out of your life for good."

"Be there in 5." She responded hanging up the phone and gathering the baby.

When Courtney arrived, Michael was out front waiting for her. He grabbed her by the hand and led her to Dr. Daniel's office. She demanded to know what was going on. All she knew was it involved Bridgette, baby Dion and of course,

Michael. "Mike, please tell me why did you have me come all the way down here?"

"Dr. Daniels, would you explain to my wife what you just told me?"

"Once again," Dr. Daniels started. "This is off the record but...Bridgette and her husband were having trouble conceiving naturally. So after months of trying, I told Bridgette about artificial insemination. After finding out she qualified for this procedure, Bridgette decided it would be best if she were artificially inseminated. She underwent the procedure and as you know, she had Baby Dion."

"And Baby Dion wouldn't have her husband's DNA correct? It would be the DNA of the sperm donor?" Michael asked verifying that he indeed was assuming correctly.

"Naturally, yes the sperm would have to come from a donor."

"Are you really trying to tell me that Bridgette got pregnant from a donation at the sperm bank?" The dumbfounded Courtney questioned.

"Yes, and it was apparently mine."

Courtney shook her head in disbelief.

"That's not even possible" Courtney refused.

"It's the only thing that makes sense." Michael argued.

"Wait," Dr. Daniels interrupted. "Michael, the likelihood of something like this happening is ridiculously small. One in a million at best."

"But it's possible, right?"

"I must admit though it is highly improbable, it is possible.

Courtney's eyes found Michael and then Dr. Daniels, still trying to put all the pieces of the story together, and then her gaze fixed on the baby.

"Tell me more." She said, wanting to know all steps of the procedure.

Dr. Daniels explained everything from how the donor is chosen, to how the artificial insemination takes place. Courtney listened and absorbed the information as best she could, while Michael was busy studying baby Dion.

Did this really happen? He thought to himself. *Is this really my son?* The words bouncing around in his mind were overwhelming. He looked at baby Dion and thought back a few years to when he was just a teenage boy sitting on the couch with his best friend. *You're going to have my baby one day.*

Michael smiled, not because he was right or because he had wanted it to happen. He smiled because if Bridgette were still alive to hear what he'd just heard, in her happy memory, they would actually share a laugh in disbelief that he had the chance to say, I told you so.

The End.

www.ingramcontent.com/pod-product-compliance
Lightning Source LLC
Chambersburg PA
CBHW021106130626
46554CB00002B/562